The Man Who Hated History

Donald Dewey has published more than 30 books of fiction, non-fiction, and drama. His biographies of actors James Stewart and Marcello Mastroianni have been translated into several languages, his fiction prizes have included awards named after Nelson Algren and Tennessee Williams, and his sports history books have been cited as being among the all-time top ten in the field.

He lives in Jamaica, New York.

The Man Who Hated History

Donald Dewey

The Man Who Hated History

Olympia Publishers
London

www.olympiapublishers.com
OLYMPIA PAPERBACK EDITION

A CIP catalogue record for this title is
available from the British Library.

ISBN: 978-1-84897-313-8

(Olympia Publishers is part of Ashwell Publishing Ltd)

This is a work of fiction.
Names, characters, places and incidents originate from the writer's
imagination. Any resemblance to actual persons, living or dead, is purely
coincidental.

First Published in 2013

Olympia Publishers
60 Cannon Street
London
EC4N 6NP

Printed in Great Britain

I admit it: I'm a nit-picker. I could claim a professional or cultural cause for this trait; after all, not only am I a policeman, but just as the speculative mind is to Paris and the clerical mind to Avignon, the legalistic mind is to my city of Rouen. Mainly though, I'm a picker of nits because I enjoy being one. If I had been a fisheries inspector in Brest, I suspect I would have been equally absorbed in poring over fins for traces of contamination. I find it absolutely delicious to detect irregularities and inconsistencies, whether they be of man or God.

That said, I must also admit that Mario Salerno's most conspicuous inconsistency was one I discovered only after he had left Rouen – and, at that, it wasn't so much a planned deception on his part as a presumption of mine he chose not to correct. Perhaps if he had corrected me, I would have never pursued the riddle of George Keller beyond a filched collection of sketches. In light of later events, I realize this doesn't reflect well on my perceptiveness, but I wouldn't be frank if I didn't admit the possibility.

Matters began, blandly enough, with the address book. Because my section is called Special Affairs, it has become something of a garbage dump for other departments. No matter the crime under investigation, if it threatens to fall outside the parameters of routine inquiry and administration, alludes to political delicacies an ambitious section chief would prefer to avoid, or simply represents one dossier too many for the allegedly overburdened, it will end up on my desk. This was not what I had anticipated that July morning four years ago when Commissioner Edgar Blanc summoned me to his office, announced my promotion, and shook my hand. To hear Blanc that day, Robert Frenaud was being put in charge of Special Affairs because of his fluency in three languages and because the section responsible for international questions required, as he put it with far too much gravity, a 'clean young broom'. For all my fantasies of rising through the Ministry hierarchy at a speed that would have made Mercury envious, I had never before conjured up one about being a 'clean young broom'. But as hapless as that job description might have been, I would have gladly settled for it if the actual work had entailed more than chasing down Moroccan street vendors, interviewing local politicians about their criteria for recommending foreign workers, and contacting the intimates of foreigners who had chosen Rouen to suffer fatal strokes or muggings. It didn't take me long to realize that my chief asset for the position was that I was 20 years younger than my predecessor, that a Special Affairs broom was otherwise always clean because it had so precious little of importance to whisk away.

All by way of saying that when my secretary, Odile, handed me the file on George Keller, with the single word SUICIDE, I grunted before the prospect of another round of letters to people who might or might not have cared about the dead man. Granted Odile had to write the letters and I only had to sign them, but after four years, the death notices above my signature struck me as some bloodless mockery in their very execution. Since there had to be an unresolved investigatory question about the deceased to merit police attention, we had to balance our announcement of the death itself with a tempered plea for the extra fact or two that would appease our bureaucratic consciences. Had your brother (aunt, cousin) been under a physician's care for the malady that killed him? Did your associate (partner, competitor) indicate why he might find it necessary to

11

frequent the most dangerous district of Rouen after midnight? Believe me, when they are sent across borders, continents, and oceans, questions of the kind sound doubly pointless. More than once I've imagined one of my cables arriving at a home in Los Angeles or Nairobi, the recipient reading it, and the recipient concluding that Inspector Clouseau had adopted the alias of Robert Frenaud. So much commotion for so little clarity.

The one consolation in George Keller's case – at least it appeared initially – was that he had left behind few people to grieve his literally precipitous end at the Hotel Flamant. As reconstructed by area investigators and confirmed by my office, Keller had arrived in France, at Le Havre, aboard the Norwegian freighter *The Northern Sky*. After two days in Le Havre, he had come to Rouen and taken a room at the Flamant. While there, his only visible contacts had been with concierge, Yvonne Belair, and a hotel guest, a Parisian student named Andre Lafont. For two days, he had been observed doing little but setting off from the hotel in the morning for long walks around the city, sitting at a café across the street sketching waiters and customers, and dining cheaply at a nearby restaurant, once in the company of the student Lafont. During the night of his second day, between midnight and one o'clock, he had jumped from the third floor of the Flamant to the courtyard, fracturing his skull and dying instantly. Based on interviews with Lafont, the concierge Belair, and others, as well as on physical and forensic evidence, foul play was excluded. The only loose thread was the dead man's missing sketch book, and I had a feeling right away that had somehow ended up in the hands of Lafont.

So why Special Affairs? For one thing, Keller was an American citizen – an automatic red flag for my section. For another, he had left behind a pocket telephone book with three foreign addresses – two in Rome and one in Copenhagen. The Copenhagen name, and one of those in

Rome, meant nothing to me. But the other Rome name – Mario Salerno – piqued my curiosity. In the 1970s and 1980s, there had been a Mario Salerno noted for his political agitation in the United States. He had been some kind of sociologist, given to creating egotistical scenes at international symposia in the name of troop withdrawals from Vietnam, ending sex discrimination, protesting Iran-Contra, and whatever the other causes of the moment had been. There had been a steady series of books too, though I was hard pressed to recall any titles from years back-scannings of literary reviews. Was it the same Mario Salerno? It was hardly a rare name. Didn't the Italians have their Mario Salernos the way the French had their Pierre Duponts and the Americans their John Smiths? Of course they did. Why would somebody like my Mario Salerno have anything to do with a suicide, whose passport described him as an artist but who had worked his way over to Europe as a seaman? Was I so bored I had to start fabricating the identities of the people receiving my inane correspondence?

No, I wasn't. So as soon as Odile walked out of my office with three signed letters to Italy and Denmark, I went back to the more urgent business of figuring out why the Greek consul needed three Algerian servants when he lived alone in a two-room apartment.

Three days later, Mario Salerno the one I hadn't needed to fabricate at all walked into my office

My first impression was of that American actor who played Perry Mason on television: in his apparently healthy sixties, tall, stocky, greying, overdeveloped jowls, a somewhat disconcerting liquidness to his eyes. I also sensed that what I had on my hands was a buccaneering intellectual between projects, somebody prying into George Keller simply because he had nothing more entertaining to do for the moment. His very look seemed to betray the transience of his interest. On the one hand, he had come all the way from Rome on the basis of my all-but-form letter and wasted little time in sounding prosecutorial for more information on the suicide; on the other hand, there was an eerie quality of glistening detachment in his eyes, even as the words issuing from his mouth approached rudeness. That first day in my office, I attributed the disconnection solely to his personality and to his impatience with me for not helping him add another intellectual credit. I have never claimed to be a perfect policeman.

"You've been in touch with the American Embassy in Paris? If Keller had a passport, he must've had a mailing address in the United States."

I told him that had been a dead end, and wouldn't have minded recalling if it actually had been. The fact of the matter was, apart from Andre Lafont and the question of Keller's missing sketches, I hadn't planned on any more conversations about the suicide and felt totally unprepared for any quiz.

"Very mysterious our Mr Keller."

"Is that what accounts for your interest in him?"

Salerno twisted in his seat so he could look doubly offended. "Are you saying you wouldn't be interested if you received the kind of letter I did? A man I've never heard of, but apparently knew well enough to remember me just before he killed himself?"

"No, Monsieur Salerno. If you say you never heard of him, you never heard of him. In your place I would have regarded my cable as some kind of misunderstanding. At most, I would have telephoned for a clarification. But come all the way here?"

"You make that sound like an accusation."

"A curiosity. Is your interest scientific?"

He smiled; mirthlessly. "Suicide isn't my field."

"But still a sociological problem."

"For people otherwise qualified than myself. But tell me about this address book. Was mine the only name in it?"

The question seemed to define a new frontier in vanity, and I was sorry there weren't three thousand names in the book rather than merely three. I had to be satisfied with his disappointed nod; even two other names seemed to strike him as unwanted competition. "I see."

"Three or thirty, Monsieur. Is it really all that odd to have the name of somebody he didn't know? I myself have a pocket notebook with the names of people I've never met. Mutual friends say I should look up so-and-so, but I haven't got around to it yet. I have other addresses taken from newspaper stories – sometimes for professional reasons, maybe from whim. Psychologists tell us clutter and insecurity go hand in hand."

"A book with three names hardly qualifies as clutter, Inspector."

"On the surface, no. But consider that Keller was somebody who wanted to get away from America for a while. An artist without money, without prospects, perhaps desperate for the job he found as a temporary seaman. Maybe he was intent on starting a new life here, maybe on travelling around the world, maybe on killing himself. In any case, a man burning his bridges behind him. He turns his back on his acquaintances in America and buys a new book as a symbol of his new beginnings."

"Very fanciful."

"Then indulge me one more step. It doesn't follow, necessarily, that the names he puts in the new book are unrelated to his past habits. Maybe the only difference is that he starts collecting *European* clutter."

He had never been called that before, but to his credit, he seemed to think it was funny. "And you think that's all that's involved?"

"As I've said, I would be interested in hearing what you think is involved. In some circles of France your reputation is not negligible. I myself followed your adventures in Montreal."

For the first time since walking in and taking the chair before my desk as a tiresome obligation, he looked at me as other than a traffic cop. "Hardly an adventure. I just think it's common sense to speak in the language of the city hosting your conference when possible."

"And I bow to no-one in appreciating the French language. But at the cost of creating an incident requiring riot police? And where was it, the state of Colorado? You deemed it 'common sense' to introduce all your colleagues by listing the government agencies sponsoring their work? Some of our own delegates were quite put out by your assiduous research."

"Social scientists should never be put out by research. But weren't we talking about George Keller?"

His defensiveness would have been more satisfying if I hadn't felt some of my own. At least Salerno had travelled from Rome for his entertainment; I had grown so encrusted with the administrative routines of Special Affairs that I had given George Keller little more thought than the tiny back-page item *Le Quotidien de Rouen* had given him. It was in that spirit that I pulled the Keller file off the shelf next to my desk and opened it out. Had I missed some obvious clue to a connection between the dead painter and the rabble-rousing academic? I wanted to think Salerno himself would point it out to me.

"George William Keller. Thirty-five. Born in New York City to parents now deceased. No siblings. Arrived at Le Havre on July 14 on the Norwegian freighter *The Northern Sky*. Left the ship at the request of the captain, Niels Barfoed. Some misconduct at sea. We have been unable to check that. *The Northern Sky* is now somewhere in the eastern Baltic. A radio message said only..." My assistant Emile Josselin's hand was as indecipherable as ever. "'Information confirmed.' Hardly enlightening on the part of Captain Barfoed, but the fault was apparently ours in putting the query in such a way he thought it adequate to reply as he did.

In any case, we were more interested in Keller's activities in France than at sea."

"On the assumption the two weren't related?"

I blamed Josselin for leaving me vulnerable to that crack. "On the assumption we are all provincials here and not the least curious about events in other parts of the world. Keller spent two days in Le Havre. He confined his contacts there to the manager of the hotel where he stayed. He then came to Rouen by train and registered at the Hotel Flamant, a place of no particular distinction one way or the other. Two days later, on the evening of July 18-19, he leapt from his top-floor accommodations into the hotel courtyard. The concierge discovered the body and had to be treated for shock."

"Just like that."

"An autopsy excluded drugs and alcohol. Otherwise, his motive was buried with him. He didn't talk much with the people at the Flamant. The concierge said he had some rudimentary French but didn't go out of his way to practise it. The only one who appears to have engaged him in substantial conversation is Andre Lafont, a student from Paris, staying at the Flamant for the summer. Lafont insists they made only small talk, where they were both from, the architecture classes the boy was taking, Keller's reasons for being in Europe. According to Lafont, Keller said he was here because he was 'tired' of America. He didn't elaborate and Lafont didn't press him. Nothing in their conversation would indicate a reason for suicide."

"Would Lafont know a reason if he heard one?"

"He's a student, but he doesn't seem especially obtuse."

Salerno gave me my smile. "So that leaves the address book."

I pulled out a copy of the passport photo we had made. "Not only that. I'm surprised you haven't asked to see this. Surely, you've come across people you know only as faces."

He showed nothing as he leaned forward in his seat to study the grainy photo. He appeared to see only what I had. George Keller was a model of anonymity. In a dark shirt, open at the neck, he could have been a social worker, dentist, or street paver as easily as an artist. His hair was neither especially long nor short, his eyes conveyed a remoteness that could have been accounted for by something as banal as a photographer's instructions. Mouth, nose, and jaw had been evened off by the original photo and erased further by the copying. It was such an anonymous photo that it insinuated an infinity of anonymities for George Keller.

Salerno shook his head and handed it back to me. "As I say, that leaves the address book."

His eyes fell to the book under my hand as the prize he had really come to Rouen for. Its bright red cover and alphabetical thumbing index distracted me, too, for a moment: It brought Keller alive in a way that none of the dusty details of the official reports did. "The other two names are of a man in Rome with an address at the General Post Office and a woman in Copenhagen."

"Your three pieces of European clutter."

I ignored his attempt to be ingratiating. "I'd say only two. For reasons quite apart from geography, the Copenhagen address has a different significance from yours and the other one in Rome. Look here. Under S we have Salerno with your Rome address. Under W we find Leo Webber at the Post Office address. But the third person, this Denise Rosen, isn't on an R page, but on an unlettered page in the back."

"That's important?"

My pedantry enjoyed his bewilderment. "You can intuit a great deal about people from their address books, Monsieur. Some insist only they can write down an address on the lettered pages an act of possessiveness, a declaration of property. Others insist on using the same pen or colour ink. Then you have the advocates of printed names and

18

addresses, as opposed to those with a preference for script. The idiosyncrasies are endless. The Rosen woman on an unlettered page, says to me Keller noted her name only out of tact. He knew he'd never need it, but found it difficult to say no."

"I thought he spoke only to this student Lafont."

"Here in Rouen. So obviously he met this Rosen elsewhere. Maybe on *The Northern Sky*."

"Well, didn't she tell you?"

My feeling of doing penance was over. "We sent her a cable, like the one you received. But neither she nor Mr Webber in Rome have shown your...whatever it is."

"And you let it go at that?"

"What do you recommend Monsieur? Are we to ask the Italian and Danish authorities to arrest the two of them? Have them interrogated until they lay bare this Keller's soul? We are not Anglo-Saxon functionaries, Salerno. We let the parish priest handle the eternal questions."

"But this woman must know something. She was close enough for him to write down her address, whatever page it's on."

"Close? I would guess a shipboard affair the seaman and the passenger, that kind of thing."

"You talk about things in bed, don't you?"

I had an image of *him* talking in bed, and felt repelled. "If they talked about why he was going to kill himself, it couldn't have been a very gay affair. All the more reason for her to throw away my inquiry."

"I think you're missing the point here, Inspector."

Josselin entered the outer office behind Salerno; if he didn't have anything more urgent on his plate, I decided, he was going to keep an eye on my Italian guest for a couple of hours. "Then question her yourself. You seem to have precise ideas about how to go about it and the time to indulge your methods. If you discover something interesting, don't hesitate to contact me. But as far as this office is concerned, the matter is closed. The American Consulate agrees with me."

It was too much of an opening, and he didn't miss it. Would I be kind enough to supply him with the addresses of Rosen in Copenhagen, Webber in Rome, the student Lafont at the Hotel Flamant, and perhaps even the shipping company that owned *The Northern Sky*? I should have said no, but didn't. The fact was, as I walked the addresses out to Odile for typing, I wouldn't have minded in the least if George Keller turned out to be more than a dull suicide or if Salerno stumbled into that fact. The worst that could happen, I told myself, was that he would waste his time and make a fool of himself. Why discourage such an outcome?

Standing near the open window of Odile's office for his cigarette, Josselin looked at me expectantly. I didn't disappoint him. He was already heading downstairs to his car before Odile began typing up the addresses. "He might resolve the investigation for you," she muttered.

"There is no investigation."

"Now there will be, now there will be."

I didn't like being so predictable, not even to somebody who had been working with me for nine years. Salerno was on his feet when I returned inside with the list. "A pity you couldn't have saved yourself this trip," I said, giving it to him. "Rome can be very pleasant this time of year."

"It's hot like everywhere else."

"But your home now?"

"Most of the year. I still spend some time in New York."

"One of these Italian-Americans searching for his roots?"

He smiled politely as he stuck the list into an inside pocket of his jacket. "Maybe that was the original idea."

"And now?"

"In search of what the roots will yield, maybe."

20

He held out his large hand, and I saw no reason not to shake it. In retrospect, I should have invented one.

Salerno did the expected. According to Josselin, he went directly from my office to the Hotel Flamant, where he engaged the concierge, Yvonne Belair, in conversation for seventeen minutes. From there he went across the street to the Café Soleil and sat sipping iced tea until Andre Lafont arrived twenty minutes later, apparently directed there by the concierge. The two remained in conversation for fifty-three minutes, whereupon Lafont returned to the Flamant and Salerno took a taxi back to his room at the Hotel Avignon.

Did I want further surveillance on Salerno? No, I didn't. But what I did want was to delve a little further into George Keller and his possible ties to our grating social scientist. Since New York was the one established intersection for the two of them, I had Josselin concentrate his queries on the New York City Police Department.

I should have known from Josselin's glumness, when he entered my office at the end of the day, that he had stumbled across something. Being of Breton descent, Emile Josselin has the unshakeable belief that France is a temporary concept, but that for him, to declare contentment about anything at any time, would risk prolonging that aberration and imperilling his region's hope for being recognized as an independent entity. As a result, he has become so dedicated to the humourless, that, no matter his professional satisfaction, he refuses to let down his guard. After working with him for ten years, I in turn have become something of an expert in interpreting the various gradations within his fixed expression. Normal glumness, the face he brought into the office after contacting New York about Salerno, was the equivalent of somebody else's war whoop.

21

As it turned out, Josselin was right, but for the wrong reason.

"At least twelve years when they were both in New York together," he said, laying out a printout with a treasure map of intersecting arrows. "Salerno was teaching at the University of Columbia. I don't see how they couldn't have known each other. They both lived in Manhattan."

I was annoyed. Four hours of tapping into every databank in France, not to mention the satellite hook-ups to New York, and the only fact we had produced was that Keller and Salerno had both lived in a city we had already known they had lived in.

"But not just New York," Josselin insisted. "Even Manhattan."

"And what's the population of Manhattan do you think? I'm sorry to break the news to you, Emile, but it's well over a million."

I didn't have to see his bulging eyes to know they were taking me in as an alien French specimen he would prove wrong as soon as he got back outside to consult an almanac. It was a good thing I didn't look too; I might have missed the notation from the U.S. Immigration Service. 'Why American Immigration;? Keller was an American."

The fleshy wedge Josselin called a thumb, came down just as I saw for myself what the notation concerned. "It's about Salerno, not Keller," he said superfluously. "He was eleven when he moved to America from Italy."

I was dismayed, but not so much that I didn't recall my remark about his searching for his roots in Italy and how he hadn't corrected me. "He was being polite," Josselin shrugged.

It was a possibility, of course, and one I brought home with me. Salerno the Polite nagged at me through dinner through Janine's petulance she had been given more canned corn nibblets than Roger, and Rachel's irritation that I had once again forgotten to bring home the newspaper. For once,

I was glad Roger shut himself into his bedroom after supper and dared Rachel to break down his door to lower his caterwauling music: It kept both of them busy away from me. At the risk of sounding more prescient than I was, Salerno's evasiveness about his nationality gnawed at me all evening. I even took it as an omen that, after making sure the children were prepared for their summer school the next day, Rachel returned to the living room and turned on an old Yves Montand concert. Montand the epitome of France for the rest of the world, but actually a Tuscan!

By the time I gave up my pretence of reading a French general's memoirs on Algeria and went up to my bedroom, I knew I was going to drop by the library the next day to brush up on Mario Salerno. My evening call-in to the office only strengthened my resolve.

"There's another thing, Inspector," the night duty man, Rolin, said after he had dispensed with the usual menu of major and minor fracases. "A clerk from the Hotel Avignon was here with a letter addressed to you."

"What does it say?"

"It's addressed to you personally."

"For god sake, Rolin, open the damn thing and read it to me!"

Out in the hall, Rachel paused on her way to the bathroom to look in at me curiously. She was right, of course: I didn't know why I was excited, either. She settled for throwing me a baleful look for smoking in the bedroom, then continued on to her evening shower.

"Not much, Inspector," Rolin reported. "All it says is, 'I never knew of the existence of George Keller before I received your message. I suppose that puts me in your debt.' That's it, sir. No signature. Nothing."

I had Rolin read it again. It wasn't really necessary; I'd memorized it instantly. What I didn't take in then, or for some time afterward, was that I wasn't memorizing a jeer, I was memorizing a plea.

It wasn't difficult finding Salerno's books in the library. I thought this a bad sign and a good sign bad because he had written so many and had induced the French state to purchase them, good because they were all still on the shelves, apparently of dated interest to Rouen's readers. Making me feel purely foolish, on the other hand, was the fact that the man had never hidden his Italian roots: They were proclaimed on the flyleaf of every single volume. Josselin had spent who-knew-how-much on transatlantic messages to come up with a particular that had been available gratis a few blocks away from the office! To put it mildly, we were going to be extremely vulnerable to September attacks from the Sûreté auditors.

For the record, I began by turning to the index of every book to look up references to George Keller, art, and New York art. All that produced were ravings about the political function of painting, the Establishment role of Manhattan gallery owners, and Salerno's conflicts with Columbia University colleagues from the Fine Arts faculty about this and that. George Keller did not exist. To be sure Salerno hadn't lied to me explicitly as well as implicitly. I then looked up references to suicide. He hadn't been lying: Aside from one or two historical allusions, he had shown little interest in the subject. I was relieved. Especially after the note from the Hotel Avignon, I wanted no banal academic explanation for his odd behaviour.

It took me more than an hour to accept that the indexes weren't going to give me what I wanted, that reading the books themselves would be necessary for gaining a firmer grasp on the man. A laborious self-indulgence on the basis of a single irregularity in our conversation? Well, I was able to rationalize persuasively enough that day in the library that George Keller had also committed merely one irregularity in the eyes of the French state and that had been enough to tie up critical resources for more than a week and to no particular gain. By indulging myself a little further, my positive angel whispered, we might justify two lines of inquiry.

To what end? That George Keller had not been the suicide thorough investigation said he had been? That Salerno knew something about the death he had been desperate to deny? That maybe Salerno had even had a hand in Keller's demise? About all these things I was still able to keep an open mind. The disturbing thing, of course, was that keeping an open mind suddenly seemed so necessary.

Salerno's first three books, published by Columbia University in New York, were orthodox sociology filled with charts, diagrams, and other kinds of statistical mumbo-jumbo aimed at demonstrating the obvious. Their common theme was European integration in the United States, the first book dealing with Italian Jews who had passed for Catholic in order to have fewer acceptance problems; the second one with the economic and political ascendancy of these people in U.S. society; and the third one with a series of identity problems suffered by the offspring of these original immigrants. To judge from cover blurbs on the third book, Salerno had attained a prominence in his field that (according to one scholar) was ,not to be confused with the faddish nostalgia of many writers who tend to reduce science to memories of the soup they once slurped in their grandmother's kitchen'. I saw no reason not to take the man's word for it.

My own jottings on these books were scant. After a couple of hours of scanning, only three noteworthy points emerged:

1. Salerno had been one of the Italian Jews in America he had written about so extensively;

2. He had been eleven when his mother had sent him from Rome to Brooklyn to live with paternal cousins; and

3. His father had died during World War II under vague conditions.

This hardly added up to a blinding illumination. But at least I was able to leave the first three tomes behind at the library with some confidence they had told me as much as they were going to. Far more relevant, I told myself, would be the later volumes I checked out and carted back to the office.

Salerno's note, on the beige Hotel Avignon stationery awaited on my desk. Meticulous as always, Rolin had prised open the envelope under the flap rather than slitting it. For a moment his caution was comforting, suggesting I wasn't the only one approaching Salerno objects as potential evidence. The moment lasted only a moment.

I put aside Salerno's note for the morning Interpol reports. From Seattle to Budapest there were the usual sightings and shootings, from Tunis to Tokyo the usual conferences. But what wasn't at all normal was an AAA alert from Copenhagen about an airport bank robbery and the killing of four police officers and two civilians. I had never seen an AAA priority from Copenhagen before, and would have bet six people hadn't been killed in the city during the commission of a crime since World War II. But as startling as the bulletin about the airport slaughter was, it also made me think of Jens Madsen and how he might be helpful in deciphering Salerno's behaviour.

Madsen and I had met at a 1997 Paris conference on 'Crime Patterns of Small- and Medium-Sized Cities'. As far as I could recall, the consensus of the criminologists, sociologists, and psychologists on hand, was that felons, who operated in smaller communities, were torn between satisfaction at being big fish in modest waters and resentment that they were inferior to their big-city counterparts. Having been dispatched to the conference by superiors otherwise engaged in such vital tasks as counting file folders, I sat through two days of this profundity in an increasingly sour mood. Jens Madsen had arrived at a far more sociable response to all the gibberish: a bright smile. He had anticipated the worst before unpacking his bag and had decided to pardon everybody from the start. It proved to be a contagious outlook. Within minutes of our first encounter at a cocktail party, Madsen, who introduced himself as 'one of those psychologists you've learned to appreciate this week', had me laughing at his mimicry of a British criminologist and Polish political scientist and conceding that I had been carrying my sulking too far.

Most of my contacts with Jens after the Paris conference had been social. Rachel and I had been guests at his home in Virum while on our way to a vacation (without children) in Sweden; he had stayed with us during a motoring trip through France; exchanges of calls, Christmas cards, and the like. The only significant professional use we had made of one another had been in November 1999, when a lunatic Dane named Andersson, managed to close himself up in the Tour de Beurre for an entire morning, threatening to blow the place up with dynamite. Jens phoned me with the vital information that Andersson had compiled a long record in Denmark for incidents related to his demented belief that he was a modern reincarnation of Norse pillagers, suggesting I use this delusion for gaining the man's trust. I did, successfully, although there were moments when both the mayor and Commissioner Blanc had looked ready to have me taken into custody for my proposal to Andersson that we go down to the harbour together to recreate the devastation wrought by the Norsemen. (There turned out to be no dynamite in the maniac's ominous looking rucksack; merely tourist brochures.)

In any case, it was Jens Madsen who sprang to mind from the juxtaposition on my desk of Salerno's books, the note from the Hotel Avignon, and the Interpol report about the Copenhagen bloodbath. To what specific end I had no idea, so I decided to phone him, explain the situation, and let him tell me what I was after. "My mind isn't arid enough to be Salerno's level, so I thought of you, Jens."

There was a long silence in my ear; I knew he was going back for a second look at something I had said. "I refuse to dignify that with a reply, Robert," he said finally. "The word that jumps out of his note is *debt*. How he's in your debt for telling him about Keller."

"Sardonic thanks are no thanks at all."

"Gratitude is that what you think he's saying?"

"What else?"

"Gratitude for what?"

"Giving him an excuse to come here, I suppose. Giving him an idea for a new book."

"But you said he hasn't shown much interest in suicide."

"So he's changed his mind. New horizons for the hungry scholar."

"Could be." There was another silence. Then: "You might be right, of course. He might have just been sardonic. On the other hand, gratitude isn't really the first definition of debt."

"What do you mean?"

"A debt, Robert, is something the debtor knows is collectible or is going to weigh over one's head."

I picked up the Avignon stationery. Salerno expecting me to collect something from him? That made no sense. "You're reaching further than I was in calling you…"

"Hush up man. This is the fun part. Perhaps the first food for thought you've ever given me. In the meantime, give me this Denise Rosen's address up here. I'll look into her as soon as I have a moment. I can't promise today or tomorrow though. Not after our little Wild West show out at the airport."

"Is it as bad as it sounds?"

"Worse," he said gravely. "The rules have been violated in our Danish Eden. Bad enough there should be a robbery and all that killing, but what we shall never forgive is the presumptuousness behind offending our sense of civilized behaviour. Let's just say the serpent is loose and we'll raze the city if necessary to find it and trample it to death."

Madsen wouldn't have approved, but I sympathized with the feeling.

Salerno's books sat on my desk the way sex magazines had once lay in my bedroom closet while I had been studying for an examination. The more I told myself they were a distraction, the more I decided they had gained the upper hand on me and it would be better to get them out of the way first. So I alerted Odile I wasn't to be interrupted for anything less than a terrorist attack on the building, shut my office door, and took to the divan with the first of the volumes I had checked out of the library.

Unlike the books I had browsed earlier, the one entitled *Ladder in the Melting Pot* had a personal edge to it. Here again was the integration of Italian Jews into America, but now reshaped autobiographically. The alternately angry and ironic tone was set in the preface, where Salerno disclosed that his original title had been *Vertical Ideations in Ethnic Groupings in America*, but that it had been changed to *Ladder in the Melting Pot,* because 'my publisher has been making considerable money lately from a journal detailing cannibal rites in Borneo'.

The book was a typical reflection of a culture in which anyone who had manned a megaphone at a street demonstration and subsequently made a second career (according to the flyleaf) out of glib spoutings on television talk programmes, had earned readers for the petty details of his life. The details that most impressed me were:

1. Salerno's father was killed by two fascist thugs on a street in Rome shortly after the boy's birth. One evening, the elder Salerno went to a neighbourhood *bottiglieria* for a glass of wine, emerged to see a wallet lying on the sidewalk, and was jumped by thugs as he bent over for the wallet. According to Salerno, this was a typical thuggery of the period, a way for the goons to show how macho they were. What passed for justice in Italy at the time determined that the elder Salerno had been drunk and that the assailants, identified as Enzo Martinengo and Luciano Silvestri, owed the equivalent of $20 in fines for 'responding with excessive vigour to a provocation'.

Although I had only Salerno's word for this version of events, I trusted his tone. When I referred earlier to the Danish lunatic, Andersson, I couldn't remember his first name was Urban. And this a fanatic who, as far as I was concerned during the siege, might well have blown me up along with himself and the Tour de Beurre! But decades after an incident that had transpired when he had been an infant, Salerno had the full names of the assailants, the amount of the absurd fine levied, and the key judicial phrase for justifying the verdict. Had he looked it up like the trained researcher he was? Had his mother been so obsessed with this parody of legality that she had drilled its specifics into his head from an early age? Possible of course. But in reading Salerno's account, I had no doubt Enzo Martinengo and Luciano Silvestri had beaten Alberto Salerno to death.

2. Salerno had an older brother named Giorgio who had been a member of the Communist resistance against the Fascists and who, at the age of fifteen, had become enough of a nuisance for the authorities to keep watch over the Salerno apartment in the hope of apprehending the teenager.

But as related by Salerno, his brother had stayed away from home until after the liberation, returning to shrug off his mother's joy with a crack about how 'if I'd been killed, you would've been told'. That insensitivity had earned Giorgio a slap across the face from his mother.

Here I had more doubts. Salerno had been six at the most when this episode was supposed to have taken place, and it was hard to believe either that he had recalled those precise words or that he had heard them from his mother later on. But this was typical of the indictments levelled against Giorgio in the book. In fact, Salerno had concentrated on his much older (by fourteen years) brother all the frustrations and resentments normally spent on a father. Giorgio had been cruel to keep his mother in anguish about whether he was dead or alive. Giorgio had been stupid after the war to oppose the cooperation policies of the Communists in the new Italian republic. Giorgio had turned out to be a sorry excuse for a human being after years of working as a real estate agent interested only in padding his pockets. The litany was so unrelenting through *Ladder in the Melting Pot,* that I made a note to myself to call Rome information for Giorgio Salerno's number. Then and there, it was still only a matter of *wanting* to believe I would need it at some point.

Then Josselin interrupted me. It wasn't a terrorist attack on the building; it was Andre Lafont, the student at the Flamant.

Lafont was still in the shop when Josselin and I walked in. The place was run by a former policeman named Roccard. During his years with the Sûreté in Chartres and then Rouen, Roccard had distinguished himself as an expert on art forgeries. With retirement, he had opened a small gallery near the university where he and his wife made the valiant gesture of showing work by unknowns, while living off the sale of prints, maps, and the like. Happily for us, Roccard had never quite lost his police instincts and kept in touch when an inquiry embraced anything vaguely artistic. The architecture student, Lafont, and George Keller's drawings were vaguely artistic.

When he saw us come through the door, Lafont seemed to consider making a grab for Keller's portfolio, opened out on the counter, and making a run for it. But then he saw something in old Roccard's eyes that dissuaded him. He was a tall carrot with small wire glasses and the kind of haughtiness that was about halfway along from superficial manner to serious substance. "I just found them," he blurted.

"Yes. And you just wanted to have them appraised before bringing them down to my office." I wasn't in the mood for any fencing, or for that matter interrogating him in front of Roccard. Preserved instincts or not, the old man was now a civilian. "You'll come with us, please."

"On what grounds?"

"I'm sure Monsieur Roccard will confirm you were seeking to sell stolen merchandise." Roccard took his time about nodding. "Sufficient?"

Josselin packed up Lafont and I packed up the portfolio. "There's something there," Roccard said, nodding to the sketches. "Monotonous after a while, but skilled."

"Thank you, Henri. If these turn out to belong to our friend here, I'm sure he'll be in again."

The old man's smile was mostly two yellowed, buck teeth. "No one is that single-minded, Frenaud. Except you of course."

I had no time for Roccard's gibes. Lafont's decision to unload the drawings irritated me, disturbed a schedule I had set out for dealing with him. Having once served as a gendarme in a summer resort town, I had learned the benefits of confronting minor criminals just as their vacations were expiring, when they were prone to becoming particularly anxious about leaving. To pull Lafont in too far in advance of his expected return to Paris, I had argued to myself, would have only provided him with more holiday entertainment. I also had a premonition that his sudden haste to get rid of the sketches had something to do with his conversation at the Café Soleil with Salerno, and I didn't like the idea of Salerno affecting anything I was doing.

Back at headquarters, Josselin hauled Lafont into the dingiest of our three interrogation rooms. In Josselin language that meant he was getting impatient with the whole George Keller affair, though I wondered if his pique was directed solely at Lafont or also included me for keeping him busy on something he regarded as minor and completed.

Lafont's initial defence was that he was entitled to Keller's sketches because he had been the American's only acquaintance in the city. Parisian snot that he was, he had already attired his moral callowness in theories about the suicide itself. "I wanted something to remember... not him, but something to remember *me* by with him. Feeling *engaged* for knowing a suicide, that kind of thing. So as soon as they took away the body, I stole the key to his room and went up to look around. He'd tossed the sketch pad behind the bed, between the headboard and the wall. I like to think he was lying there that day, wondering if he had the energy to go downstairs to the café to do more drawings. He looked over the things he'd done, saw how meaningless they were, then tossed the pad over his head and went to the window. He married art, the marriage went kaput, and he got a divorce, that's why he killed himself."

Josselin didn't miss the part about 'stealing the key'. While he went back to clarify whether the concierge, Yvonne Belair, had surrendered the key to him, I looked at the drawings. There were about thirty sketches in all. Old women, students, Café Soleil waiters, tourists, a mailman. Each had been drawn as a variant on an expression I thought of as agonized firmness. Keller's pencil had been pressed down so hard it had all but perforated the paper, but there was also tremulousness in the hand, weaving in and out of the faces like a car without a brake. And drawing after drawing, it was the mouth that dominated, small mouths, big mouths, tight-lipped mouths, open mouths, toothless mouths. Each and every one of them seemed to be telling me something, but I couldn't understand the words.

Josselin interpreted my study of the sketches as a sign I didn't give a damn if the concierge had given Lafont the key or not; he was right. "So you intended bringing these drawings back to Paris with you," he said testily. "But then Salerno comes along, and you change your mind and decide to sell them. That what he advised you to do?"

Lafont shook his head, but more nervously. "I didn't say that."

"Your conversation with Salerno at the Café Soleil had absolutely nothing to do with going to Roccard?"

The boy looked at me in appeal. "What are we talking about here, Picasso's hidden treasure?"

I've always thought lies enter a room as noxiously as the stink from a toilet; I smelled a lie. "For you they might as well be Picassos. Stolen property is stolen property."

He made the mistake of shaking his head into his chest, giving Josselin an excuse to grab him hard under the chin and jerk him back up to attention. "Look at the inspector when he's talking to you!"

"Are you two crazy? Okay, they're Keller's. Yes, I went into his hotel room and took them. So what? Cops never put their hands on things at a crime scene? Tell me another one."

Josselin flared, but I admired Lafont's bravado. It was sullen, far too outsized for him, but still there. "Let me put it this way, André. If you want to get out of here anytime soon, you're going to go over your little chat with Salerno for us. Leave out a comma and it will be a very long time before you look at an architectural rendering in Paris, or anywhere else."

He finally seemed to join us in the room. "You're not interested in the drawings! This is all about Salerno!"

"Wrong and right. What did you talk about?"

It wasn't until halfway through his tale that we arrived back at the lie I had smelled. It wasn't what I had expected, but how can you rely on lies being what they should be?

"He said he knew something about suicide, he'd studied it or something. I said that was nice. I didn't really want to talk about it. Then he asked me if I'd ever sailed across the Atlantic. I said no. He said he found it odd an apparent manic depressive like Keller, could sail through that graveyard of thousands of suicides over the centuries and not feel compelled to take a dive. I said I knew one better, had he ever been to Le Havre? Every knife and fork in Le Havre feels like it's been greased. It combines the best virtues of Channel fog and French provincialism. But Keller had also been there for a couple of days without being tempted."

"What did Salerno say to that?"

"He agreed with me. Said it was strange Keller ignored all those atmospheric aids until he got to Rouen."

"What else?"

Josselin's glower had discouraged him from reaching into his shirt pocket for a cigarette before, but he was suddenly so shaky with his thoughts, he didn't care about retaliations. I gave him a light. "We, I guess I mean me, I turned the conversation to Rome. I was there a few weeks ago and I wanted to talk about that instead of what he was reading in my face."

"What was he reading, Andre?"

His exhale seemed to be for a lifetime of petty guilts. "Keller's sense of place. What I said before, about how he was on the bed and then went over to the window just long enough to block out *where* he was! When he could abstract himself from his surroundings. When he could look into a deep, dark well and see absolutely nothing. No hotel room, no courtyard, no ledge, no Flamant, no Rouen, no France, no nothing!"

I was aware of Josselin staring at me for a translation of what Lafont was going on about. Only one thing occurred to me. "You didn't go into that room after the drawings. You went there to try it yourself."

He nodded readily, a shame dissolved instantly by acknowledging it. "A minute inside and I knew how he'd done it," he said, removing his glasses and lowering his weak eyes into his shirt as he polished the lenses. "The bed, the drawings, the window, I tried imagining it down to the tiniest detail. But nothing, Frenaud! I knew how he'd done it, but that didn't mean I could do it. The stupidest things kept coming into my head. *Place* things. A memory of being depressed at the *lycee*. A horrible afternoon walking around Montparnasse when my sister died. Things I tried to summon up to get me in the mood, to help me emulate Keller, but they actually eliminated any chance of me succeeding. There were too many associations, too much interference from the outside world." He put his glasses back on. "Even in that room of death, even as I was trying to recreate everything, I was still just a student on a holiday. A tourist. It would all pass eventually, and I'd go back to Paris."

"Doesn't sound like something to regret to me," Josselin said.

Lafont's bravado was back. "Exactly what I don't. I don't have any more time for adolescent pangs about the romance of a suicide. Salerno convinced me I didn't need that kind of souvenir from here."

"How did he manage that?"

He seemed surprised I didn't know. "He understood exactly what I was talking about! He'd tried it too, he said. I was no special case. I couldn't even be unique in my adolescent gloom!"

I could have put Lafont in a cell overnight for the drawings, but his admission seemed to earn him the Flamant's sheets for the evening. So I treated him as the naughty student he was, sending him off with instructions to report back to my office the next morning to sign a statement about the theft. Josselin went off to deal with a robbery at the harbour offices of the International Red Cross. I went home with *Ladder in the Melting Pot.*

Rachel had already fed the children. As a peace offering for not calling to say I would be late, I stopped off at the only kiosk in the district open after six to buy another copy of the morning paper. I also made sure to turn to an inside page so she would accept the paper as mine and not make another crack about extravagant spending.

Most of Rachel's protests about my spending have to do with, what she regards as, my social-climbing recklessness where Roger and Janine are concerned. Just as my father had insisted I devote a month of my summer vacation to the International Institute for Advanced English Studies, I insisted Roger enrol in a similar school a few blocks away from where we lived. Always vigilant against Roger being favoured over her, Janine had worn me down with demands that she also be allowed to attend the school (where for children her age the courses were more along the line of advanced play). Frankly, I was gratified both children took to some educational structure during the summer. In my day, the summer had meant the freedom to kick around a ball, to build impossibly intricate model airplanes, and to devise a thousand other impromptu solutions to a hovering boredom; when my father had announced he expected more from me than that in the month of July, I had done a lot of sulking, even a little crying. In Rachel's eyes, my reaction had been more rational than Roger's or Janine's. At the same time, though, she could hardly discourage them from wanting a supplementary education, so she sublimated her feelings into anxieties about the family budget. I wanted to spend so much on the summer school? I thought it would be to Roger's benefit to be in the same classroom with the mayor's son and the daughter of the Liberal Party representative for our district? Fine, but that was going to mean one newspaper a day, generic brands of soup instead of the English kind I liked, and two omelette dinners a week.

That evening was an omelette night. It might as well have been egg shells for all the attention I paid to it. My mistake had been in glancing at another page of Salerno's book while riding in the elevator up to the apartment. The truth was, he and I lived on different planets. First, he had lost his father to the beating incident. Then his brother had gone from being a frightening absence to a brooding, embittered presence. Finally, with the boy still shy of his teen years, his mother had not hesitated to walk down to the American Consulate on the Via Veneto to use the very existence of her older son the Communist militant as a 'bad influence' argument for allowing Salerno to obtain a visa to study in New York. Compared to that kind of childhood, I thought, my protests about having to attend summer school had been an incredible self-indulgence.

"It was the times," Rachel said, unimpressed. "The mother was smart enough to know the Americans just had to hear the word *communist* to do strange things."

"Strange? Accept a mother's denunciation of one son so she could ship another one across the ocean?"

Sometimes, Rachel's black bangs seemed to frame her within a windshield; she was in the car on her side of the glass with mature human beings and I was outside on the road with the naive tribes. "Do you think it was so different in Algeria? My cousin's family was whatever was convenient. Algerian, *pieds noirs*, Jews, whatever it took to get along with the people in their district. It's called survival, Robert."

"This was Italy, not Algeria. Nobody was throwing *plastique* into cafés and markets. This woman took it upon herself to *beg* the Americans to help Salerno to get away from his own brother!"

"Years ago, decades ago. People you don't even know."

"It was still wrong."

"This from you?"

"I'm not talking about politics. Today or then, it's still wrong."

She started to say something, thought better of it, then stood up to collect the dirty plates. "A tactic. And did it work?"

Of course, it had. According to Salerno's book, anyway.

When I moved in with my cousins in Brooklyn, I was astonished to discover I had a beautiful, dark-haired cousin named Patricia. She was two years older than I was and, more painfully than for other members of the family, had been forced to walk a gauntlet of nuns to pass for being Catholic. I suppose it was inevitable her initial line of defence was to take on the social strategies of her parents as a theological mission, becoming more Catholic than the pope; or, in the words of the neighbourhood wise-guys, becoming the Virgin of Pineapple Street. Later on, Patricia resorted to more radical defences, but when I first met her, I couldn't imagine anything more effective than her ugly white stockings, neck-high dresses, and obsession with explaining to me the difference between plenary and partial indulgences.

When I wasn't thinking about Patricia, I was working to improve my English. And here I came to the conclusion that neither native Americans (for discouragement) nor Patricia's family (for

encouragement) offered a reliable yardstick for gauging my progress. Then I found the criterion I was looking for, at the St. George Playhouse. It was an American film with the Italian actor Vittorio Gassman. He was playing an immigrant, but fatuously enough that his English was Joe Bananas with the cadences of Laurence Olivier. For months, I followed that picture around Brooklyn, downtown, out to Bay Ridge, Bensonhurst, wherever the paper said it was playing. I must have seen it thirty or forty times, saving every penny I came by to be able to compare my vowels and consonants with Gassman's until his were clearly inferior.

But my real Americanization came with baseball. A couple of weeks after my arrival, the Brooklyn Dodgers were in the World Series against the New York Yankees. At first, I suffered silently through the family's endless arguments about who was going to win. But this was hardly an adequate defence, not with even Patricia holding fervid opinions about it all. In fact, it was as difficult to avoid talk of baseball at my cousins' table as it had been to skip politics at supper with Giorgio in Rome, and the more I had to listen, the more my dumb politeness and ignorance soured into the irritation I had felt during my brother's tirades. This was especially so at the mention of Joe DiMaggio. DiMaggio had recently retired but was still the hero supreme for my cousins, despite the fact that he played for New York instead of Brooklyn. Or maybe I should say *because* he did, since playing for New York fulfilled the distance requirement for idols. Joe DiMaggio was *up there* not just up in the Bronx, but over what the family had come to recognize as an altar. He was the model guinea to have made good and he was worshipped ardently by those uneasy with their own native deities.

For me, though, Joe DiMaggio was mainly significant as the presence that had replaced Leon

Trotsky for supper benedictions. As a result, I became a Brooklyn Dodger fan, as in fact I had developed a fascination for Stalin back in Italy. I didn't pay much attention to regular-season games; I took it for granted, sometimes stupidly, that the Dodgers would win enough of those to qualify for a World Series against the Yankees. My only concern was the opportunity for seeing the DiMaggio icon levelled. I never quite attained that goal: When Brooklyn finally did win in 1955, DiMaggio had long been gone. That semi-victory in the books, I lost my interest in baseball.

"The light, Robert. It's late. What are you reading?"
"About American baseball."
"Very exciting, I'm sure. The light. Please."
I lay awake in the darkness for almost an hour. Even now I can regenerate in my nerves my growing sense of vindication for not having simply forgotten about Salerno the moment he had walked out of my office. And the other thing I recall from that night was finding Rachel's foot with my own and leaving it there deliberately, feeling the space between her third and fifth right toes and wondering how the mother of our children could have ever been so unthinking, even as a twenty-year-old, to go on a motorcycle in her bare feet. Nobody should have ever been so young and irresponsible, I told myself.

The next morning, Andre Lafont was waiting for me like a good little boy on the hall bench next to my office. His anxiety and indignation seemed to be in the right proportion, so I said nothing to him as I went inside.

The day's first order of business, at least to hear Josselin, was the pilfering of the Red Cross offices the evening before. The problem seemed to reduce itself to the Swiss nationality of the office supervisor and his adamance about trusting only his safe to keep more than 25,000 euros. It wasn't the first time we had been up against this Alpine mentality, and, as Josselin went through the particulars, we both knew what was coming. Before the morning was out, there would have to be telephone discussions with the local head of the French Red Cross, with the head of the International Red Cross for France in Paris, and probably with the Swiss Embassy in Paris. They would all assure us of their faith in our investigative abilities, we would urge them (again) to keep their money in a bank, and they would allude ever so tactfully to the hundreds of IRC offices around the world where staff funds could be kept in a floor safe without fear of being taken. The possibility of an inside job by a Red Cross staff member? Such things were never contemplated, or at least not until the culprit had been identified and packed off back to Geneva.

"What else?"

Unfortunately, there were several elses, and I listened to Odile, Arnaud, and Brunel detail them for me. But because their reports didn't include a single word about Mario Salerno, I found the usual morning litany unbearable. As Brunel relayed the latest Customs warning about privateers who had taken over the Czech arms trade, I wondered if I wasn't keeping Lafont on the hall bench too long, risking some unwanted shift in his mixture of edginess and arrogance. I also thought of Jens Madsen. Had he found the Rosen woman, got her to say anything useful?

Finally, my fortitude was rewarded, and I cleared out everybody but Josselin. He thought we were going to talk about some suspect he had zeroed in on for the Red Cross robbery, and didn't look remotely interested in the fruits of my overnight reading of *Ladder in the Melting Pot*. "We have no crime except the drawings," was his dull response.

"You're so sure Keller was a suicide?"

"Do you have a reason to doubt it?"

Of course I didn't, and Salerno's yellowed memories about growing up in Brooklyn, New York, couldn't change that. But then I played back what Josselin had said, *no crime except the drawings*. "And if there was another one, having nothing to do with Keller or his drawings?"

"You're ahead of me, Inspector."

I laughed for him; the idea was suddenly enthralling. "Meaning miles behind you. But I'll overlook your condescension. Think a moment though, Salerno comes all the way here for a reason that defies common sense. He has no intellectual agenda, whatever he told Lafont to get him talking. The only people he talked to were me, Lafont, and the concierge. No ulterior motive for coming to Rouen as Rouen, either, with Keller just a convenient excuse. Ergo, Emile?"

"Back to Keller."

"And?"

"I don't know," he sighed.

"Something he felt jeopardized when Keller killed himself, maybe?"

"By Keller killing himself?"

I could almost hear the clicks behind his hooded eyes. "Excellent, Emile! An important distinction, jeopardized by the suicide act or merely by the knowledge Keller was in Rouen?"

"And this crime in question?"

For that I needed my first cigarette of the day. "Keller arrived in Europe on a ship," I said, awash in nicotine. "Smuggling something, say. Drugs? Maybe more of these confidential documents Salerno's shown a talent for procuring and waving around in public?"

"From a third-rate painter?"

"Okay, forget the documents. Let's just say Keller was carrying object X for Salerno. That's why he staged an incident aboard *The Northern Sky,* to get himself cashiered at Le Havre. We have to get more information on that, by the way." Josselin didn't jot a letter in his notebook. "And remember: He stayed in Le Havre two days for no apparent reason. Maybe he was waiting for someone who didn't show up?"

"Salerno?"

"A thought, but after two days he becomes agitated. Maybe something has happened to Salerno and will happen to him, too, if he remains any longer in Le Havre. So he comes to Rouen, a secondary assignation. But again Salerno doesn't show up, on time, anyway. Our painter becomes even more desperate. He realizes that whatever he has been counting on getting from Salerno, money, for example, in exchange for object X isn't going to materialize. It drives him to his final desperation and act of folly."

Poor Josselin. Although it was hardly the first time I had begun his day with a fantasy about an on-going inquiry (frankly, I relish wallowing in my shadow plays), I knew I had crossed the line imposing Keller and Salerno on him. Fortunately for both of us, the warming excitement from my first cigarette began receding. "All right, back to reality. Give Lafont two minutes of your time. If he hasn't remembered anything useful, send him back to the bench, prepare a statement about the theft of the drawings, have him sign it, and leave him alone again for about a half-hour. Then have Odile or Arnaud or somebody pass by and wave him out of the building as offhandedly as they can. The least we can do to the self-important little bastard, is make him feel a little less significant to world events."

As soon as Josselin left, my eye dropped on the leather bookmark protruding from *Ladder in the Melting Pot* on the desk. I told myself to ignore the bookmark and open the book to any page, that whatever I read would be my sign for the day. What I read was:

I loved being in New York, loved being in America. But what I loved especially was being a foreigner there. Since everyone anticipated the worst from me, the smallest knowledge of their place was treated as a tremendous achievement. When I took the right subway, I was congratulated for my sense of adventure. If I gave somebody the proper street directions, I felt personally responsible for mapping the city. I could do no wrong because *I* was wrong, and every move from that state of original sin was viewed as an act of universal rebirth. I was deemed worthy of salvation every hour of every day. I was in a direct line from Adam, the Prodigal Son, and Richard Nixon. I was found by the Americans to be eager for another chance.

My own next chance came later that morning. I was returning to my office from Commissioner Blanc's weekly review with the sector chiefs, when a familiar voice froze me near Permits and Licences: "Robert! You've become too important to say hello?"

Margaret Tierney, a plump blonde who took hallways and the people in them like a tank, was the administrative coordinator for the U.S. Consulate. Years before, she had approached Rouen as the first step on a career journey toward Paris or the French Desk at the State Department. But then she had fallen in love with a local attorney of some standing named LaSalle and had redirected her ambitions to a family and the stability of her consulate position. As I quickly recalled, seeing her advance on me, she had a son in his teens and two younger girls. "How are you, Margaret? More chaperoning?"

The frail stick of a man standing before the Permits clerk was clearly a new arrival from Washington, in need of all the shepherding Margaret had become expert at. "Maybe a little undernourished," she winked. "But Mama Tierney will whip him into shape."

"I thought it was Mama LaSalle."

She rolled her eyes on cue. Over the years, we had fallen into assigning each other exaggerated characters. For me she had become WHAT MADE THE U.S. CONSULATE WORK, for her I was THE MALE CHAUVINIST ALWAYS ON GUARD TO PRESERVE TRADITION. "I took Jean's name in front of a priest, Robert, not before all the printers who gave me business cards and a desk placard."

"And how are your children putting up with that?"

She told me. But as I prepared to answer what would surely be a similar question, I remembered one of our first conversations, at least five years before when one of my duties had been vetting French nationals hired by local diplomatic offices. We had been reviewing the credentials of a former university student who had once been arrested demonstrating outside the local offices of an American oil company but who, less than a year later, was looking for a job at the consulate. Among the other arguments Margaret had deployed to allay my suspicions, was an admission that she too had once been involved in street demonstrations. "One time I was even handcuffed to a Columbia University professor," she had said. "How's that for education?"

I couldn't wait for her to stop complaining about her teenage son to remind her of that remark. Yes, she did remember telling me that story. "That professor you were handcuffed to," I asked, not daring to hope, "it wouldn't have been Mario Salerno by any chance, would it?"

Margaret Tierney's curiosity turned to delight. "No, but he was there, too. The one I was cuffed to was named Klein. English Literature."

"Did you know Salerno?"

"Everybody did. He was one of the few eggheads there who didn't take the last helicopter off the roof of the Saigon embassy. He was always finding new things. The environment, gays, that business in Cyprus between the Greeks and Turks. Allende. He was even in some feminist things, though God knows he had another reputation."

"What do you mean?"

"Women, Robert. You know, the breed that cleans the house and does the laundry while you're having fun here?"

"A ladies' man?"

"The modern vocabulary would call him a Salerno man."

"I see." And of course I saw nothing.

"He used to be a friend of a friend. She used to tell me stories. What's so important about Salerno? He coming here?"

I shook my head quickly; it was the truth (he wasn't *coming*), and I saw no reason to spread my tics into American government circles. "His name came up on the fringes of a minor matter."

She didn't believe me completely, but she still had her job. "Look, I better get back inside and make sure my charge isn't signing his salary away to the French state. We'll talk later. Maybe I can tell you a thing or two."

"I'd appreciate that."

Returning to my office, I promised myself I would forget about Mario Salerno and George Keller until Margaret, not I, called. If my chief assistant had been anyone but Emile Josselin, I knew, my fixation would already be around the building. So for the next couple of hours I applied myself to the stupidities of Red Cross office supervisors, Liberian seamen who got rolled by prostitutes, and South Korean importers unable to account for nine hours on freighter trips through the Mediterranean.

Then Jens Madsen got me back to essentials.

"I think you should speak to Denise Rosen, Robert."

"She's there? Put her on."

"No, I mean you should come up here."

"You're joking, Jens!"

"Salerno wasn't. He came up here straight from Rouen. He spent last evening with Rosen. In every meaning of the term."

I was flabbergasted. In how many ways was Madsen's announcement infuriating? A simple phone call to the Hotel Avignon or some airline would have prepared me for the news that Salerno had gone to Copenhagen instead of Rome. Not only was the man grating personally and politically, now he was also a Casanova! "I'm happy for the great romance, Jens. But what does that have to do..."

"I've spoken to her," he cut me off sombrely. "Got her in on a pretext about checking the papers of foreigners because of the airport mess. Salerno frightened her, Robert. I'm sure it has something to do with your suicide."

"But you just said they even screwed!"

"As far as Rosen is concerned, that was just one of the things he seemed to have in mind."

What could I say? That my prejudices about Salerno were supposed to exist only in my head? That they could hardly justify running up to Denmark with all the real problems littering my desk? And what about even the permission from Blanc to go off like Don Quixote? Had Jens Madsen lost all sense of proportion?

"I think you should think about it," he said. "There's no emergency. Salerno's already left again and she's up here studying Kierkegaard in the original. That should keep her safe and stupefied for twenty years."

It was a relief to hear his laugh. And to feel a choice about going or not going to Copenhagen receding.

"Meanwhile, I'll e-mail you some particulars about our little chat."

"Express mail would be better."

He understood immediately. "Ah, still nervous about acting on our intuitions, are we? The big bad Blanc might wonder if Robert had a brain?"

"Express mail, Jens."

"I hear you, I hear you. And I'm the last one to criticize anyone these days. Maybe it's just the atmosphere up here since that damn shooting. People are walking around like these thugs have robbed them of their souls. Everything was so orderly before those bastards started pulling the trigger."

"No, it wasn't, Jens."

"No," he sighed. "No, it wasn't. Why do you think we're always ready to give thugs and terrorists so much credit?"

"Better to credit them than blame ourselves?"

"Sometimes I know why I like talking to you, Robert."

I paid for that compliment the rest of the day. I ordered a ham sandwich from the café on the corner and ended up with a loathsome piece of anchovy on a hard roll. Arnaud walked in to announce he was resigning to take a position with his father-in-law's security firm. Rachel called to say that Roger and two of his friends had been caught smoking in the toilet of his summer school. My call to Margaret Tierney, well, *one* of us had to initiate it, was an exasperating adventure in Consulate switchboards, secretaries, holds on the line, and, finally, dropped lines. Finally, on my third attempt, I got through. I was already expecting Margaret to ask what I wanted when, instead of an hello, she said simply: "Mario Salerno." I lighted my second cigarette of the day in gratitude.

What Margaret told me came from a one-time room-mate in New York named Jill Faber. Faber had apparently been Salerno's student, lover, and co-star in street demonstrations in the 1970s. Even after so many years, Margaret seemed able to recall the nature of each and every one of the protests attended by Jill Faber, oppressively so. "Margaret, I'm sure it was once a vital issue to have more women teaching at Columbia…"

"Now, now, Robert. I'm giving you the opportunity to be educated as well as informed."

"Salerno was in these protests, is that your point?"

"He could hardly not be after spouting off on the subject. Jill was really infatuated with him. She said he was a typical man, but with possibilities as a human being."

"Enchanting. Who was he, Margaret?"

A pause. Then: "Somebody out of his depth."

"Excuse me?"

"When Jill told me some things, I just wrote him off as a phony. Salerno the Intellectual Rebel sure helped him sell books…" Odile stood in my doorway signalling something; I waved her out again. "…But I don't think that was fair. In time alone the hours he put it…"

"Point taken. But how was he out of his depth?"

"With the other things," she said, as though it should have been obvious. "The quack stuff with his cousin Patti."

My eyes ran to the book on my desk. The cousin Patti had to be the one described as the Virgin of Pineapple Street. "I'm listening, Margaret."

"One I remember was a fat guru named Shinman. He was this slick conman who caused some attention years ago for some quackery he called Naturopathy. And he was just one of many."

I felt like I was getting further away from Salerno than closer to him. "One of many what, Margaret?"

"These woo-woo people Patti brought around. From what Jill said, Patti was always higher than a kite. A burned-out case, always looking for Nirvana with the latest holy man."

I tried again. "What does that have to do with Salerno?"

"Everything! See, cousin Patti would suddenly turn up and he'd take her craziness as seriously as he did what was happening in Chile or Angola. Shinman, for instance, talk about cynical! He convinced his followers the way to solve the abortion question was – yes, now it comes back to me, was to think of it as foetal euthanasia."

"Are you mad?"

"*I'm* not. I'm telling you what these Naturopathy freaks believed. The way they had to approach abortion, Shinman told them, was to approach the foetus the way they would have the terminally ill. That way you skipped all the debates about when a foetus became a human being. Naturopathic Courage, that's what Shinman called it."

"And Salerno went around endorsing this?"

"That's what I'm telling you, Robert. He'd accept it because cousin Patti did. No matter how screwy the idea, if it came from Patti, he seemed to turn off his mind and go for it. Then when Patti moved on to another lunacy, he'd move on with her."

"So when you say he was out of his depth…"

"Where Patti was concerned! He was like some hick determined to impress everyone how 'with it' he was. Like a fool who keeps snapping his fingers at jazz so you'll think he's cool. The rest you can figure out."

"Rest?"

"The womanizing, Robert! After she met Patti, Jill never felt like she was alone with Salerno. And she was ready to bet she wasn't the only one."

I hadn't seen any of this in *Ladder in the Melting Pot*. "We're talking about… Patricia Mariani here, right?"

Margaret laughed. "I think so. Why not ask Salerno?"

"I told you. His name just came up…"

Another laugh. "The key to a persuasive liar, Robert, is being able to persuade yourself first."

I put the receiver back down softly, as though that wouldn't alert Odile to the fact that I was ready to listen to what was on her mind. Outside with my secretary, I thought, were normal investigations that could be frustrated only by the lack of a perpetrator, weapon, witness, or all three. With George Keller, on the other hand, something even more vital was missing, the crime itself. In fact, the only thing I really had was the perpetrator.

I would like to say my decision to go to Copenhagen was an inevitable result of investigative logic, but that wouldn't be the truth. My superstitiousness was as much of a factor as anything else.

As Rachel would be the first to attest, I have developed a practical belief in all the minor voodoos. If the first cigarette of a new package has been rolled less than firmly, I'm sure I'll lose the whole pack during the day. If two acquaintances appear in the morning paper's necrology, I'm certain a third will expire somewhere in the world before midnight. I can't drop a fork without expecting a visitor, I avoid walking under ladders, and I've been curious enough about folk tales to ascertain, through assiduous study, that only black cats with a spot of white on them pose a danger. I'm not proud of these dreads, but it has seemed the better part of discretion to accede to them.

My superstitiousness where Salerno was concerned was aroused by my chance meeting with Margaret Tierney. Her connection to Salerno, tenuous as it was through their mutual friend, seemed like an omen I was going in the right direction. My destination? I still had no idea. But I did commit myself so far as to have Odile look into flights to Copenhagen.

In the meantime, Salerno wasn't alone; felons from around France chose Rouen as their summer playground and foreigners as their victims. Only a few days after the robbery at the Red Cross, the assistant office supervisor, one Francoise Mann, was found shot to death on the kitchen floor of her apartment. Josselin and I were still on that scene when we were summoned to a café robbery on the other side of the city. Matters there had got out of hand when the café owner had brandished a gun, leading to his own death, that of one of the bandits, and the wounding of three patrons. My luck, the wounded were all members of an Irish tour party. That same day, two idiots from Verneuil got into a squabble about the woman they had both pursued into my jurisdiction. When a Pakistani textiles dealer objected to their flashing of knives in front of his store, he received a blade in the chest for his trouble. By the time the ambulance arrived, the Pakistani was dead and the neighbouring shopkeepers were screaming about 'French animals'.

If all this didn't make for the worst day I had ever had, it was close enough. Making it more onerous, was that I was in no rush to get home to hear more of Rachel's recriminations arising from Roger's dalliance with tobacco and the bad example I had set the boy. My one moment of serenity was listening to Josselin and Brunel going out the door of the outer office shortly after six-thirty, leaving me completely alone. Even the abandoned computers and overflowing wastepaper baskets, that I could see through the windows of the other offices around the central courtyard, seemed to invite me into a peaceful after-hours world of their own. I couldn't help thinking of my childhood fantasy of being locked up overnight in the endless toy section of Leroux's department store.

Instead of toy tanks and Zorro costumes, however, I had to entertain myself with the daily *resumé*, which Odile always compiled as a final task before going home. The *resumé* was a transcribed summary of everything that had been accomplished (or not accomplished) during the day. In theory, it was a paper monitor of our daily enterprise, to lurk in the files as a potential indictment of our failures; in practice, not even Blanc gave it more than a few seconds before tossing it in the garbage. As he had once put it to me privately, anybody who needed the *resumé* to know what he or his colleagues were working on, needed a transfer to some less taxing avenue of employment.

What the *resumé* was not supposed to contain was an important item of new information. But to my dismay that evening, that was exactly what it did contain, hidden within a summary of Josselin's activities for the day:

E. Josselin, crime scene, Francoise Mann; crime scene,

Café Beaucaire; office, Francoise Mann; computer room,

Patricia Mariani; crime scene, Mehta Textiles.

I was furious, and determined to take it out on the drawers of Josselin's desk if that was where he had left the computer room printouts. As I stormed out of my office, I beat off all the justifications for Josselin's behaviour that occurred to me. He had got so bogged down in the killing of the Red Cross woman and in the café shooting, that he had simply forgotten to tell me the New York police had sent him something on Salerno's cousin, Patricia Mariani. He hadn't wanted to weigh me down with still another matter on the day. He had been dissatisfied with the information from New York and intended getting back to them in the morning. I accepted none of those possibilities. The one and only reason I had needed the *resumé,* was to find out about the Mariani printouts, I was certain, that Emile Josselin regarded George Keller as a dead issue and wanted me to think so, too.

At least he hadn't hidden the printouts: They were in his WORKING box atop his desk. Camping down with them in Josselin's chair, I had the makings of a book on my lap. Patricia Mariani had been papered for more than thirty years, and what the New York authorities hadn't recorded, the police departments of Boston, Baltimore, Washington, Chicago, Duluth, Memphis, New Orleans, and San Francisco, as well as FBI bureaux from the Atlantic to the

Pacific, had. The misdemeanours added up to a copy of the penal code: vagrancy, shoplifting, driving without a licence, drunk driving, possession of chemical substances, damage to public property, damage to private property, loitering, abuse of a public official, on and on. Under the heading of disturbing the peace alone, I counted 23 violations, some apparently stemming from political demonstrations, but others arising from the complaints of neighbours, automobile drivers, and fellow train passengers. Sprinkled among the misdemeanours were the felonies: two assaults on policemen, possession of a dangerous weapon, and four instances of dealing chemical substances. Given such a *curriculum vitae*, I was appalled to add up no more than ten months of actual time spent behind bars for the woman and mostly in fifteen and thirty day clusters related to the disturbing the peace charges. Either Patricia Mariani had always had the services of an astute attorney or the U.S. legal system was the modern definition of forbearance.

Be that as it may, this was the woman who, according to Margaret Tierney's friend, had beguiled Salerno. How? With what? Whatever else Salerno might have been, he was a man with a modicum of intelligence, somebody whose concerns probably had value even for some people with a finer sense of personal responsibility than he himself had usually displayed. Nevertheless, here he was in the throes of somebody whose life read like the caricature of an over-aged beatnik. Was this the net result of all the horrifying pains and sacrifices that had gone into sending him across the Atlantic after the war, somebody who had wandered from state to state, from youth to middle age, seeking nothing but her own bizarre pleasures? How could even Salerno have continued to patronize such footloose stupidity for so long?

I had no idea. But by way of consolation, on my second scanning of the printouts, I discovered what I wanted to believe was Salerno's link to George Keller. The only list nearly as long as that of Mariani's infractions, was the one itemizing the jobs she had held when taken into custody. On fifteen occasions, she had been associated with galleries, art supply shops, or other enterprises having to do with painting. Was it possible Salerno had missed that connection, that it had probably been Mariani who had given Keller his address in Rome? I couldn't believe the calculating man who had sat in my office was that unreflective. Salerno had simply lied to me by not raising the name of Patricia Mariani.

But a lie wasn't a crime. Nor were the half-uttered fantasies Denise Rosen had apparently tantalized Madsen with in Copenhagen. Only my obstinacy insisted on one final step before accepting common sense and closing the Keller matter once and for all. I left a note on Josselin's blotter instructing him to ask New York for information on the present whereabouts of Mariani. I would have felt an incompleteness if I hadn't done so.

Back in my office, I still didn't find much enthusiasm for going home to Rachel's disapproval, so I finished off the dregs of an Italian brandy that had been dying in torment in my bottom drawer for three years. For an omen-looker, the opportunity to get rid of an old bottle like that, with all the insinuations of out with the old and in with the new, was momentous. In that frame of mind, I went over to the couch for one last fateful stab at *Ladder in the Melting Pot*. I landed on Salerno's account of the events of July 1, 1976, the night he tried to kill himself. That, too, seemed appropriate. I would never know what had helped George Keller succeed in his death, but at least I would find out why Salerno had failed.

I hadn't felt like a foreigner in America for some time, so there were no more daily rewards of being applauded for pronouncing my diphthongs or for

knowing that Fifth Avenue divided Manhattan's east and west sides. On the other hand, there were continual reminders I wasn't a bona fide American, either: the need to recount my life story to a clerk whenever I applied for an official document, to speak glibly about Italy whenever somebody penetrated my biography, to scamper to a dictionary or encyclopaedia when some conversational reference went over my head. Instead of easing such banalities, my years in America made them more oppressive. It was as though my every conscious effort to adapt had also propelled some antagonistic force never to do so. Socially, the result was appalling. I became clumsy, intrusive in my silences, aggressive in my attempts to be invisible. With everybody in every situation, I came to go, only that. My abiding sensation was of never being in the right place, although I had no idea where the right place was. I doubted it even existed. I couldn't imagine a place where other people were more than limitations, where someone else had *exactly* the same dilemmas I had, where admissions and arguments didn't leave the enervating feeling that I had expressed fewer facets and complexities of my personality than I really possessed. I couldn't conceive of a place where the progress of months and years didn't mean merely the accumulation of insurmountable barriers to things I had to prove to myself, for myself. In militating against anything at all that even vaguely resembled hope, my sole activity was communicating my iron bleakness to others so they could share it with me.

Finally, I panicked twice over. I'd always hated the bathroom in my West Side apartment. The lighting was bleary no matter how strong the medicine cabinet bulb, the floor tiles always seemed cracked even though they were perfect hexagons. But that afternoon, after hours of soap operas I had watched one after another without rhyme or reason, it struck me that I belonged in the bathroom   just sitting on the edge of the tub to be one with the dimness of my mind. I didn't even need to shut the door for isolation; as soon as I perched on the rim of the tub, I was sealed off from the rest of the apartment and everything beyond it.

I don't know how long I just sat there staring at the tiles and pipes. What I do remember is that I imagined nothing. I didn't need to because everything I required was in front of me, under me, behind me. Tears, feeling of any kind   all that was beside the point, extraneous. I thought about people, then I dismissed people. I resented nobody, blamed nobody for anything. When a face sought to take form in my head, I banished it without commotion. Refreshment was reduced to turning my body a few inches so my back could hold off a draping numbness. I became so good at it, so totally abject, that even as the idea began demanding attention for itself, I knew I didn't need the Valium in the cabinet. And that was when I panicked the first time. I gave my own gratuitousness a pass, gave it its head so it could be more unpredictable than my own. On the rim of the tub, with the Valium in one hand and a glass of water in the other, I ordered myself to focus exclusively on rationing my sips per tablet, to dissolve the gummy, powdery taste in my mouth thriftily so I wouldn't have to stand up to get more water and feel some part of my body collapsing. The only race I entertained, was between emptying the Valium bottle and emptying the glass. Even the race of life against death felt ludicrously irrelevant.

That same appreciation of the ludicrous saved me and brought on the second panic. With both the bottle and glass empty and a beer keg about to erupt up into my chest from my stomach, I managed to hang on to the sink and stare back at the cabinet mirror. Only laughter, I told myself, could relax the pressure. But if I were sane enough to be able to laugh at the ridiculousness of taking the pills, why hadn't I been sane enough to avoid making a spectacle of myself in the first place? The only conclusion was that I had done something far worse than try to kill myself: I had been fatally incoherent.

Somehow, I got to the living room phone. An operator listened calmly and mechanically. I hated her, and slammed down the receiver with a vow to make her pay for being the first to learn about Salerno the Suicide. I managed to yank a jacket off a hanger in the hall closet and get the elevator down to the lobby. For some reason, there was a cab discharging a passenger right in front of my building. The driver seemed disappointed I wasn't bleeding from some major artery ("I don't see nothin', buddy"), but got me to the hospital, seven blocks away, without encountering a red light. The hospital interns disapproved of my throat for their cold tubes. The Latino cop forced to record my statement in the emergency room practically twisted his nose off the bone not to smell the vomit all over my shirt. The staff psychiatrist was mainly relieved I was a respectable person with significant contacts in academic psychiatric circles. Each and every one of them disabused me of anger, despair, and other oppressive emotions. Salerno had undone himself in an irretrievable way, and that was all there was to it.

I laughed a great deal in the hospital; to myself, but loud enough for all that. What else could I have done? I laughed in the spirit of somebody watching Buster Keaton being thrown out of a skyscraper window: No question the immediate reality was serious, but other scenes would surely follow. *That* was my real despair. I had spent decades arranging my life according to one self-image, and now, after merely one afternoon and evening, that image had fallen away like a sliver of dead skin. On the one hand, my industriousness in creating the rambunctious personality of Salerno had been revealed as vain; on the other, here I was already on the move again, recognizing the challenge to start from scratch again. Could I do it?

I knew only I had the answer to that. But just how did somebody remake himself a second time?

Charles Caron lived within a flinch of the Gros Horloge, on a broad avenue in one of those high-rise pastel mazes city planners had favoured in the 1950s. Arriving on the scene, I found Josselin in complete control. He had pinpointed Caron's apartment as the leftmost patio overhang on the second floor, had stationed Brunel at the back of the building to keep an eye on the fire exit, and had drafted two neighbourhood gendarmes to accompany us inside. I left one of the uniforms in the lobby just in case.

As I took the steps to the second floor ahead of Josselin and the second gendarme, I had every confidence we were about to resolve both the burglary at the Red Cross and the murder of Francoise Mann. We had identified Caron as the man who had been seen in public with Mann for the better part of a year, had established he was the same Charles Caron who had once served three years in Nantes for burglary, had learned from one of Mann's colleagues that the woman had been in distress about her relationship with Caron, and had discovered that Caron had settled substantial bills immediately after the Red Cross robbery. The only remaining problem, it seemed, was ensuring that Caron came peacefully.

He did, and didn't. As soon as I identified myself at the door, Caron, a slight blond with the face of a ferret, bolted back inside the apartment. I already had my weapon out, and heard the officer behind me releasing the safety from his, as I barrelled through the door after the fool. What followed over the next few seconds was absurd. One moment Caron was hurrying toward the divan in the sitting room, the next (as I shouted a warning) he was veering off toward a table where he had left a pair of pants just brought home from the tailor's. Even as I was assuring myself he couldn't have a weapon under the pants, Caron grabbed the hanger, whirled back to us, and began swinging it as though he were Douglas Fairbanks manipulating a sword. From the corner of my eye I could see that Josselin, his weapon aimed directly at Caron's stomach, was as befuddled as I felt.

We waited until the pants fell off the hanger to grab the idiot and manacle him. Only with my blood thawing and returning to my veins did I wonder if there had been some rationale behind his frenzy. Josselin was ahead of me. While Caron sulked about the tightness of the cuffs, Josselin went over to the divan, tossed aside a cushion, and uncovered the murder weapon in the Mann case, a Smith &Wesson .38.

Josselin used a pencil to extract the revolver from its hiding place. As he brought it over to me for a closer look, I suddenly had the feeling that something familiar had just happened, that Caron's reaction to our arrival was something I had experienced before, and recently. I tried to piece it out as we looked around the apartment for other evidence:

A. His first reaction had been to run to the gun for defence.

B. His second reaction had been to realize he stood no chance against us and, moreover, would be leading us directly to the murder weapon.

C. He couldn't have just stopped in the middle of his alarmed run to the divan, since that alone would have been enough to direct us to the gun, so he had grabbed for the first object he had seen, however ridiculous, in hopes of distracting us from his original destination.

What did that add up to?

Not merely subterfuge, I told myself, finding only clothes in the bedroom bureau; *panicked* subterfuge. Charles Caron had been forced to improvise *desperately*.

Mario Salerno had been much calmer, to the point of that eerie disconnectedness in my office between what his eyes and words wanted. He also lacked Caron's blond hair, and was probably thirty years older and a hundred pounds heavier. But all those differences admitted, I didn't find it strange to wonder how George Keller had been Salerno's wire hanger.

I took the lead in the Caron interrogation. I had little choice, since Blanc had made it clear he (and the army of Swiss officials on his back) expected Caron to be our priority until we had obtained a confession. To reinforce his concern, the Commissioner descended from his eyrie twice during the afternoon to monitor the interrogation, then lingered again for almost twenty minutes before going home in the evening to his *col vert*. My luck that it was during this last interlude that Jens Madsen called from Copenhagen. As I stepped from the interrogation room to get the call, Josselin looked up from behind Caron with an expression that said he had expected better of me. Blanc caught the look, didn't know what it was about, and seemed to prefer not knowing.

I took Madsen's call in the hall outside the interrogation room. "Denise Rosen came by again this morning," he said without preamble. "She wanted to have a coffee, said she was feeling stymied making friends in the city and I was as good as it got. She wasn't making up that part altogether. Anyway, this time she came right out and said she thinks your friend wanted to kill her."

Arnaud came down the hall and began making hand signals to ask if he should relieve me in the interrogation room. I looked through him. "*Thinks*? Doesn't she know?"

"I don't think she'd be able to swear to it in a courtroom, no."

Arnaud looked quite capable of waiting for my answer until it was time for him to join his father-in-law's security firm. I finally waved him back to his office. "Look, Jens, I have to say you've been describing a very impressionable woman to me…"

"I think you should talk to her, Robert. I really do."

The first time he had said it, it had still sounded something like my idea; this time didn't. "You really think there's something going on?"

There was a Madsen Silence. Then: "Going on. Or, gone on."

In retrospect, it might have been the only answer that would have persuaded me. "In a day or two," I decided aloud.

Blanc stood before the interrogation room like a guard lacking only a halberd. He dabbed at his moustache with a middle finger, rocked back on his high heels, and glanced down the hall to make sure nobody overheard his impatience. "I assume this is as urgent as wrapping up Caron?"

"The American who killed himself at the Hotel Flamant?"

He needed a moment to remember. "What about it?"

"It may not be that simple. I'll probably have to go to Copenhagen for a day to interview somebody."

"There are indications of foul play?"

"It's involved," I fenced. "But I think we have to look into it."

He tired of rocking on his heels and waiting to hear the precise reason he should be indignant. "If that's what you have to do, Robert, that's what you have to do," he said, looking at his watch. "But not before Caron is tied up with every bow in the building. Understood?"

I couldn't have engineered a better trade-off. In exchange for getting Charles Caron to sign a statement about deeds that were incontrovertible, I had my superior's official acknowledgement that I had been right to keep after the Keller-Salerno connection.

Charles Caron broke within twenty-four hours, and broke pathetically. No sooner had he confessed to the murder and robbery, than he sought frantically to recover his lost terrain, first by implicating Francoise Mann in the Red Cross theft, then by claiming she had attacked him in her apartment and he had been forced to shoot her in self-defence. The miserable performance ended only when Caron's attorney suggested he was worsening his situation by slandering the dead woman.

With Caron out of the way, I was free to rail at Odile for not having supplied me with the travel information to Denmark I had requested. The information she dropped on my desk an hour later promised a journey of hellish proportions. Whatever the straightforward maps of Europe said, the only way to meet with Denise Rosen was to take a 6:30 flight from Rouen all the way down to Lyon, wait there for more than an hour, fly back up to Paris, wait another two-and-a-half hours, then finally fly another two hours to Copenhagen. "In other words, even Air France wants to remind us we're in some little backwater here!"

Odile thought I deserved such an itinerary for my earlier tone with her. "As long as we hold on to our own self-importance, Inspector," she sniffed. "Me, I would take the train to Paris and fly from there."

Having strained relations with my secretary, I doubled my losses by summoning Josselin and hitting him with all my grievances over the way he had been moping through the Keller investigation. "The *resumé* isn't where I should be discovering what you've been up to! I'm beginning to get the idea you're doing me a favour by working on it!"

There was the smallest glint in Josselin's eye as he rearranged the marbles in his jaw to reply. "People like this Caron," he said, deliberately refolding his legs in the chair before my desk, "they follow a textbook. They want something, they reach for it, we reach for them. One, two, three. This Salerno, we have no clue what he wants and we don't know if he's reached for it, is reaching for it while we watch, or will reach for it tomorrow. But we keep reaching for him anyway, the third step without the first two. Maybe I'm not used to working that way."

"And you think I am?"

He shrugged, as ever, making it seem more like an indulgence toward the company than some personal concession. "Maybe you're more flexible about some things, Inspector. Maybe that's why you have your position and I have mine."

I waited. Words hadn't worked, I thought, so maybe silence would. It seemed to take forever, but finally he continued: "You don't like Salerno. He makes you nervous about something I don't think has much to do with this painter. Ever since he came here, you've been waiting for him to lead you somewhere. First to Lafont and the concierge at the Flamant, then to the woman in Denmark, then to this other woman in America. If I thought he was the criminal you seem to, I wouldn't let him lead me anywhere. I'd be there ahead of him to make sure he doesn't commit a crime."

"But without hard evidence…"

It was as close as he ever came to a smile, and he had to gaze at his big knee to cut it off. "I was always told it's a bad idea to let prejudices and preconceptions get in the way of the job," he said. "That's unreal, of course, but at least it's good to know what the prejudices are." He took his time lifting his eyes back to me. "What are yours toward Salerno?"

I had no doubts about that, even if Josselin was the first I admitted it to. "He's irresponsible," I said, wanting him to share my anger, even for a second. "A whore on the American marketplace. The man went through too much to end up being satisfied with just that."

Josselin let my heat subside before he opened his mouth again; he sounded suspiciously kind. "When the doctor slapped me on the arse and handed me to my mother, he didn't say, 'Here, Madame Josselin, here is a bright new boy who will one day grow up to be the chief assistant of Inspector Robert Frenaud in Rouen.' There are things that come after that we have no control over. Maybe I ought to have worked in the rail yard with my father. Maybe you should have been…"

I had to laugh at my sudden vulnerability. "A clerk," I said, smelling the fresh paint in the rear of the Leroux Department Store from the evenings my mother had brought me around to pick up my father. "A store clerk who rose to supervisor. Don't laugh. That was an important position. It meant my father was eligible for a twenty per cent discount."

"On toys?"

"Especially on toys."

He tucked away his smile with a nod. "So you didn't become a clerk and I didn't end up chasing hooligans away from freight cars. And Salerno, he didn't become the responsible person you think he should have. What of it? How can that be anybody's business but his own? Where's this crime? And there's something else." He shifted in his seat more uneasily. "There is talk. The usual riff-raff gossip. That you've been under pressure. That you've been doing odd things. Maybe you've been staying here late because you're in no hurry to go home. Even that you've taken to drinking alone here at night."

I was stunned. The only drinking I'd done in the office had been to finish off the Italian brandy. Were even the cleaning women watching me?

"Like I say, riff-raff talk. Not important in itself. But you don't want even that drifting up to Blanc."

"Let it," I said, determined to try with him one more time. "Last week, Emile, there was only person, me, who believed there was something wrong about Salerno coming here. Now I think there are two others in Denmark. All I need from you is your usual efficiency for another couple of days. And no more worrying about my reputation with Blanc, *mon ami*."

He was startled by the personal address, then embarrassed for having betrayed his surprise. He sprang to his feet just to have something to do. "Then we should see what New York has found out about the cousin today," he said awkwardly. "I haven't checked yet."

We were both relieved when he hurried out the door. Another minute and I might have started grilling him about the office swine who had decided I hadn't been eager to go home recently.

I called Rachel and asked if she wanted me to pick up anything on the way. She said a pack of cigarettes for Roger.

Even substituting the train to Paris for a bizarre Rouen-Lyon-Paris flight, I felt washed out when my plane finally landed in Copenhagen in mid-afternoon. The first sign of the city's trauma over the airport robbery came at the immigration gate: Even with Madsen standing a foot behind him and muttering into his ear, the thick-browed officer parsed every word of my ID printed by the French state. Past the control gate along the mezzanine, there was an automatic weapon at the ready every twenty yards, and that was without counting the ostensible travellers working undercover. But these responses I could understand; what airport *hadn't* been blanketed by security in the wake of the September 2001 attacks in the United States? What surprised me was that the cause of all the tension, the bank branch where the four policemen had been killed, was still shuttered and being guarded as though billions of euros still lay in its vaults.

"By mutual decision," Madsen said, seeing my expression as we walked past. "Neither the police nor the bank wants people coming off a plane and touring the place like it's Tivoli."

"So why advertise it like Tivoli?"

"Shock has its own timetable, Robert."

I didn't know what that was supposed to mean, but I kept quiet until we had reached the parking lot and Madsen's dusty red Volvo. He looked as well as I had ever seen him: His weathered, salmon-like face seemed to have been exposed to the sun more than once lately and he had all but eliminated a paunch that had been sneaking up on him. But he had also darted looks at everybody we had passed between the terminal and his car, as if daring somebody to act suspiciously.

"I've arranged a meeting at a coffee house at five. I told her you wanted to talk about Keller. One thing should lead to another so I didn't see any reason to bring up Salerno."

"Or what she assumes she told you in confidence?"

"Something like that," he said, pulling out of the parking lot.

"'Something like that.' What's going on, Jens?"

He shrugged. "Like you said on the phone, she's impressionable. Start with facts. Everything will be on solid ground that way."

I didn't think that answered anything. And for somebody who said he had met Denise Rosen only twice in the formal setting of his office, he sounded unusually protective.

"Don't always be a cop, Robert," he smiled as the SAS skyscraper came into view miles away.

"That's what got me here."

"Granted. And when you leave again, I'll still be 44, I'll still be having a middle-aged crisis, and I'll still be thinking about the possibility that Denise Rosen will help me weather some of the shoals."

I didn't want to believe him; it wasn't only unprofessional, it bordered on the unethical.

"Like hell," he said easily. "She's part of your investigation, not mine. And we are sure there is an investigation, aren't we?"

If I could have done it and still arrived in the middle of the city for the appointment with Rosen, I would have demanded he stop and let me out so I could walk the rest of the way. How many times had I reassured myself on the train and plane that, if nothing else, I had persuaded Jens Madsen that Mario Salerno was proper police business? And I hadn't been the one to pull myself out of the interrogation room with Charles Caron with a story guaranteed to get me to Denmark. But instead of an investigative ally, I seemed to have found another wayfarer drawn to the rocks by the Siren of Kierkegaard. Keller, Salerno, and now Madsen, Denise Rosen seemed to be reducing my inquiry to a collection of melancholy men eager to pull off her bra and panties.

"That's better," Madsen said when I laughed.

"It was ironic laughter."

"We recognize no other kind in the land of the fairy tale."

69

We had time for Madsen to make a stop at his office behind the Radhusplads before going on to the coffee house. While he went up to check his messages, I stayed downstairs, in the mild late afternoon breeze, to get used to my legs again. Maybe it was the absence of Josselin and his reliably glum expression, but I felt I had taken over the role of disapproving presence. I disapproved of trains, planes, and cars that cramped the muscles. I disapproved of the German couple taking turns at photographing one another before the Radhusplads. I disapproved of the flimsy instincts that had drawn me away from what was surely more urgent business, both in the office and at home in Rouen. How dare the Danish students walking past look so unconcerned about the cop killers in their city, not to mention one of their officials fucking one of my key witnesses!

When Madsen came back down, he looked amused to see me pacing so sternly. I saw his point.

The coffee house was a short walk away on Ostergade. His professionalism hadn't been completely compromised by Rosen: The place was a colourless, square room below the street that did little business for its cakes and sweet buns so late in the afternoon. Only two of the dozen or more tables were occupied: one by a pair of businessmen hovering over a laptop report on Wall Street stocks and the other by an elderly woman working on a crossword puzzle. It was as discreet as a public place could be.

We were a half-hour early and Denise Rosen was twenty minutes early. The way she locked eyes with Madsen in greeting one another made me think they had just completed a round in some private game he had won. Since I didn't want to believe that had anything to do with telling me about their relationship, I asked her what she wanted from the waiter and from Kierkegaard. She told me twice as much as I wanted to know.

"It's beyond me how anyone can claim to understand a genius like that without reading him in the original Danish!

And you know why so few make the effort? Because they're more interested in their academic careers than in Kierkegaard! There's nobody else to read in Danish, so they tell themselves it's a waste of time to get into it for one measly philosopher. That's why they stick to the translations. It's the laziness of academic social climbing!"

Sweeping at loose wisps of her honey hair, Denise Rosen rushed on, anger at others and excitement with herself fuelling her ardour by turns. I couldn't help thinking she was put together like a Chinese box game, with the boxes out of order. Her thin voice was too small for her big body, her body was too outsized for an austere Dane brooding by candlelight through the Nordic night, and the halting energy of her words came nowhere near illuminating the great metaphysical ambitions behind them. Did she have the patience to rearrange the boxes one day so that one could slip smoothly into the next larger one, creating a seamless whole? I had no idea.

"You're giving me the same look George did," she said, her monologue finally exhausted. "Like I have two heads."

"Keller said you were foolish?"

"Not in so many words. He was polite. Like you."

"Maybe he was learning something."

She had more on her mind than tactical politeness. "I have to tell you, Inspector, when you sent me that letter, it was like somebody had been eavesdropping on my thoughts."

"You expected Keller to kill himself?"

"More like imagined it. But what was I supposed to say to you? 'Thanks for confirming my fantasies, Inspector Frenaud. Our relationship could have only ended in the way it did?'"

"Relationship in what sense?"

She hesitated, maybe for Madsen to interrupt and tell me he already knew about all that and would fill me in later. But he pointedly picked up his cup for a sip of coffee. "I had no idea how spooky the Atlantic was," she relented. "The moon shines like ice, the way it has for a zillion years, and that's all there really is. It scares you, makes you feel insignificant. The last thing I wanted to feel leaving the States and coming here on my authenticity quest was insignificant."

"Excuse me for saying it, Mademoiselle, but why you went to bed with George Keller isn't the reason he killed himself."

She was offended. "Maybe they aren't all that separate, either!"

My allergy to American egocentrism ran up and down both arms like a rash. "Why not? For all you know, Keller was the kind of erotomaniac who liked frustrating women in bed. Or maybe he was Casanova and just didn't like your style."

She blinked in alarm, but then Madsen's deep-chested laugh made her smile. "Tell Inspector Frenaud about Le Havre, Denise. How Keller came to be marooned there."

She thought about reaching for her coffee, and I would have liked to believe it was because she was there to make an official statement. But I had no such illusion when she changed her mind. Props like coffee cups were for uncertain people, and she had long since bottled what she had to say. "When we stopped trying to prove something to one another, he asked me to get some cognac from the steward. It took some doing because it was late, but the steward had a daughter and assumed he knew why a woman might need cognac to put herself to sleep. Next morning they found George roaring drunk in the passenger lounge. Before they could get him to his bunk, he took a swing at the first officer and threw up all over the place."

"Did you talk to him afterwards, when he knew they were going to leave him at Le Havre?"

"It didn't seem to bother him all that much," she nodded. "He even thought it was funny he was being left in France on Bastille Day."

"So he didn't mind not going where he planned to."

"Where was that? He never mentioned any special destination. The ship was going to Bergen, so he was going to Bergen."

I prayed Madsen would remain silent. "Are you sure? We found two addresses for Rome."

She showed nothing. "I don't think that meant anything."

"You knew he had them?"

Her crossness was back. "You just told me he did. I was talking about him on the ship. I don't think he was planning itineraries to Rome or anywhere else then."

Madsen finally put in his oar. "What Inspector Frenaud is trying to grasp is why, if Keller had no particular destination in mind, Mario Salerno acted as though he had."

"Did I say that, Jens?"

"No, I suppose you didn't," he retreated. "Why don't you just tell the inspector what happened when Salerno came here."

She looked disappointed in Madsen. "Jens told you about that?"

"In broad outlines."

"It's so nice to feel part of an Interpol connection."

Madsen snapped something in Danish. Whatever it was, she turned her blue eyes back on me in resignation. "We had what I thought was a very pleasant evening. We met for a drink at the Angleterre, we had dinner, then we went to a jazz club. Mario was very entertaining, knew almost as much about Kierkegaard as I did. Or at least he was entertaining when he wasn't asking a million questions about Keller. When we left the jazz club, we went back to my apartment. Call me an idiot, but I was sure he was as grateful for my company as I was for his. May I have another coffee, Jens?"

She fell silent while Madsen waved futilely to the counterman. Only when he got tired of signalling and stood up to take his order over to the counter did I understand the pause: She thought it more delicate to speak with me alone. "We fucked all night. Is that what you wanted to hear?"

"If that's what you did."

"Until seven in the morning. And then we slept until noon, woke up, and did it again. Until I nodded off."

"So he didn't tell you anything of interest between seven and noon."

It took a moment, but she cracked a smile. "That's right."

Madsen went off to the toilets in the back; I was as glad as she looked. "All right, now tell me about this fright you had. Yes, Jens told me. And to be perfectly frank with you, I'm here as much because of that as because of what might have happened on *The Northern Sky*."

"This is more about Salerno, isn't it?"

I remembered Andre Lafont coming to the same discovery in the interrogation room. "You're the second person to catch me out on that. But yes, it is."

"I hope you have better luck than I do."

"Pardon?"

Her pale skin accentuated the red embarrassment in her cheeks. "You know, how a woman might sometimes compliment a man? Well, I did the shoddy thing of comparing him with my great tryst on the ship. What else should he have wanted to talk about than that? But not Mario Salerno. He just saw it as an opening to get back to the other people on *The Northern Sky*, the other passengers, crewmen, officers. I got really pissed. I was tired of talking about George. I wanted to forget about him. But Salerno kept prodding, wanted to know if I was the only friend he'd made aboard. The last thing I remember in my boredom was mumbling and nodding off in his arms."

"Mumbling?"

The waiter brought second coffees for everyone; I reassured myself I was still two behind from where I would have been in Rouen.

"I woke up again about twenty minutes later," she said, once the waiter had gone off again. "We weren't snuggled up anymore. He was sitting at the edge of the bed staring off at the window. I felt disoriented. Then I realized it was because my head was on the sheet and my pillow was now on his lap. He looked so silly sitting there like that, like he was suddenly Mister Modesty and had to cover himself up. I said his name, and he looked back at me not at all surprised I was awake... No, more than that. It was like he'd been having a debate with himself about something and I took the place of one of the debaters in his head. Just slipped in there like I personified whatever that half of his brain was arguing. Does that make sense to you?"

It didn't, but I nodded. "What's this you said about mumbling?"

"I'm getting to that," she said impatiently. "He was... well, he was erect again. I reached over for him, and it took the longest time for him to forget about the pillow. But he really didn't want to make love again. He looked so damned... mournful. And then he asked if I'd been lying to him, if he had really made me forget my experience with Keller. It was such a ridiculous vanity, but something told me not to laugh. I mean, he's not a young man. He can't expect... Anyway, I just said yes, and he kept staring at me like he was counting off seconds for a test to see if I was lying. Then he asked me what the name was. I didn't know what the hell he was talking about. He said before nodding off I'd mumbled the name of somebody Keller had been close to. That did it!"

Madsen slid back into his seat with a wince at the sight of the second coffee served to him.

75

"I got so mad he wouldn't stop with Keller! I told him I forgot the name, it'd probably come back to me, but right then and there I had to get ready for a day at the library."

"And he just got dressed and left," Madsen said.

She nodded. "I wasn't going to tell him that name if his life depended on it. Enough already!"

I felt a chill at how close she was to the truth: A life *had* depended on it, but not Salerno's. "And there *was* somebody on the ship close to Keller?"

"Johnny Stuck," she said readily. "A member of the crew. Everybody called him Johnny Sticks. A Dutchman." She shook her head in bewilderment. "Okay, we weren't Bogart and Bacall in *Casablanca*. But I really wouldn't have minded opening my eyes and, instead of more questions about Keller, hearing how he'd just spent the greatest night of his life with me."

I jotted down Stuck's name. "So he never found out about this Dutchman from you?"

"He found out on his own." For once, Madsen looked as unprepared as I was, and she couldn't resist touching his wrist apologetically. "I didn't get a chance to tell you. Salerno called from Rome around noon. He asked if Stuck was the name I'd mumbled before dropping off. I told him it was and that I really didn't want to hear from him again unless he could keep Keller and his friends out of the conversation. He said nothing. Just hung up."

A police car went braying past the coffee house. Not only Madsen, but the two businessmen, the crossword puzzle lady, and the counterman shot tense looks out the window. That left me to say something to Denise Rosen's open hurt of a stare. "My personal view, Mademoiselle, is that you did well to do what you did."

"Jens told you... ?"

"Your feeling he might have killed you? Yes."

"I really don't think I'm exaggerating, Inspector. The way he sat there with that pillow, like he was debating if he should smother me with it. And that robot way he looked back at me when he knew I was awake..."

I pretended to make another important note or two until she excused herself from the table and went back to the ladies' room. "That mumbling probably saved her life."

Madsen had come to the same conclusion. "He wanted Stuck's name. But for what, Robert? Just so he can go around and talk to anybody Keller ever knew? What's he after?"

"Something worth killing her for. And maybe something worth killing this Johnny Stuck for. We better call Amsterdam."

Madsen nodded with a glance at his watch. "Didn't you say there was another name in Rome, too?"

I hadn't exactly forgotten about Leo Webber, the address at the General Post Office. It had just smacked so much of transience, the tourist passing through, the student needing a place to collect another cheque from his parents for financing his travels, that I hadn't counted all that heavily on Salerno catching up to him. But, of course, Madsen was right. Josselin would have to alert somebody in Rome. That didn't seem like much of an oversight next to the feeling that, with Jens, I had somebody truly working with me. Not on the George Keller case, but on the Mario Salerno case.

I tried to be tactful about getting out from under Madsen's plans for me for the evening. No, I didn't want to stay at his house in Virum, I wanted any hotel room in the city where I could collapse for a few hours. And no, I certainly didn't want to be a third at dinner with him and Rosen; all I could see that leading to was a lot of awkwardness at the end the evening before I either travelled to Virum by myself or he reluctantly put his desires on hold for another night and accompanied me home to the suburbs. It seemed like a solution by acclamation when he found me a room in a small hotel near the Norreport Station and agreed we should meet for breakfast the next day. When he dropped me off in front of the hotel, Rosen couldn't have been happier about getting out from the back seat of the Volvo and taking my place next to the driver.

I postponed thoughts of dinner until I showered and put in a call to Rouen. Josselin had already gone for the day but had left a message for me with the night duty officer Rolin. Cousin Patricia Mariani had not been seen in New York for more than two weeks; friends had told the New York police she had been planning a trip to Europe. There had been no specific mention of Salerno or Italy.

I hung up, annoyed with myself for not having the crew and passenger list from *The Northern Sky* with me. Had it been as simple as that? Had cousin Patti been on the ship with Keller, igniting some jealousy in Salerno? I didn't believe it. My brain wasn't *that* addled. As soon as I had read the name Mariani the first time, I would have remembered the list of crew members and passengers I had scanned after first looking at the Keller dossier. Even sitting on the bed of my hotel room on Frederiksborggade, I clearly recalled names like Eth and Bruch and Carlsson; there had been nothing remotely Latin, let alone Italian, on the list.

I dismissed the idea of calling back Rolin, having him rouse Odile at home, and having her come in to find the ship list. That much could wait twenty-four hours until I returned to the office. And yet I didn't want just to nod off before the heaviness that gripped my legs and insisted I didn't really have to eat at all. I had already justified my trip to Denmark with Rosen's story and the possible threat to Johnny Stuck? Fine, but I could have done more, *should* have done more. When all was said and done, I still didn't have anything to present to a magistrate as a definite crime.

I went back to *Ladder in the Melting Pot,* after Salerno's suicide attempt and immediately after his mother's death. I could almost hear him congratulating me for making the right choice.

In the wake of my mother's heart attack, I decided to spend more time in Rome. I moved into the apartment I had bought for her and gradually came to think of that place as my home as much as my Manhattan apartment. Left to my own devices, I would have made an exemplary revanchist, the egghead equivalent of the Abruzzo migrant who returns home in retirement after thirty years as a construction worker in America, tosses off the occasional anecdote or English expression to impress his neighbours, but is basically grateful for being able to reclaim his familiar beginnings. This was not to be, however. The fact is, I felt like almost as much of foreigner in Italy as I had in New York.

Mind you, I didn't lament the feeling. I liked being treated as a visiting luminary, solemnly and ceremoniously. In America I had been patronized; in Italy just about everyone but my brother Giorgio waited for me to patronise them. I was an accessible version of the United States, the Cinerama experience with the subtitles conveniently provided. I had come from the same place as the intelligence agencies that had manipulated decades of Rome governments, as the aircraft manufacturers that had corrupted armies of local political leaders, as the financial mandarins who always called for wholesale layoffs for salvaging the economy they had butchered. I was a report from the front for the politically combative and ideologically exasperated, as well as for those (often the same people)

who wanted to hear greater details about Clint Eastwood. I was sought out as someone who knew first hand whether there were practical hopes for dreams and practical reasons for nightmares, as a representative of what others were contemplating doing, didn't think they had the nerve to do, or were sure they would never sink to doing. In short, I was an ambassador: deemed worthy of respect even in dispute, a sharp edge to round tables, a smooth addition to canapés and wines, and a foreigner. No matter the claims of my birth certificate, I had spent too many years not shopping for grapes at the Campo de' Fiori to be able to slip back within its stalls and umbrellas inconspicuously.

Why have I exploited this situation rather than contested it? Most immediately, because there is little I can do to smother natural curiosities about an America that has relentlessly extended its social walls, economic flooring, and political aeries over the last half-century and more. I also have to eat. And third, I am not a foreigner to myself.

Call it a survival formula, dating from one of those mornings I awoke in that New York hospital with the morose realization that the Mario Salerno I had invented for myself, had been fatally compromised by my bout with the Valium bottle. There would simply never be a happy ending for my attempt to be all things to all people, PLUS something else to those not in the immediate vicinity. In New York, I had wanted to be a New Yorker, as indigenous to the place as the Brooklyn Bridge, while also holding out a piece of myself as Salerno the Roman. In Rome, I indulged every prerogative accorded a *professore* as my domestic right, while winking at my New York reserve that none of the deference was to be taken seriously. In both situations, of course, what I was actually saying was that *I* shouldn't be taken all that seriously, an admonition that, when I finally let it penetrate after my suicide attempt and my mother's death, was especially spurious. Too much had been invested over the years for the making of nothing more than a mental tourist.

And so I created my personal atlas of frontiers and territories: the Land of Salerno. However arbitrary in conception, once established, it was a solid antithesis to the whimsical. As long as I was in the United States, that was who I would be, no interior reassurances that I was more than my given place. Vice versa, when I was in Italy, I was indeed only there. In the Land of Salerno, the marked territory of the moment was also the only territory; its frontiers existed to define its limits, not to imply the other lands beyond them. In this way, I discovered, I was able to be with people truly and fully, not merely with shades that seemed to waft off elsewhere for insidious comparisons and contrasts. This new outlook permitted me to travel 180 degrees from the oppressive feeling that I was always and solely coming to go, always and solely seeking a right place I wasn't all that convinced even existed. I felt finally at peace, so much so that not even the artificial nature of my cartography (never disguised from me) was threatening. On the contrary, the artificial was part of the consolation.

A raw throat was waiting for me when I opened my eyes again. Whatever traffic had been in the street below before I had nodded off was now gone; a lone car horn sounded blocks away. I threw Salerno's book off my chest and looked at my watch. It was after nine o'clock.

I sat up with the line 'the artificial was part of the consolation'. Did even Salerno know what it meant? If the name of a reputable American publisher hadn't been staring up at me from the spine of the book, I wouldn't have thought it possible for such gibberish to find its way to a commercial press. The monomania was absolutely clinical. Allowances made for the man's language, I had encountered similar involutions only in the statements of confessed felons with mental problems.

So why wasn't I feeling even more vindicated I was on the right track?

I went over to the window thinking about the call I owed Rachel. I always phoned her after flying somewhere, but it had been more than six hours since I had arrived in Copenhagen. For all she knew, I was still up in the air being hijacked to Syria. Or worse, she had assumed I had landed safely, hadn't given me another thought, and was now camped down on the couch in front of the television. I didn't like encouraging so much nonchalance. It had already been three weeks since we had made love. What was I aiming for, three months?

The shops along Frederiksborggade were closed for the night, but it took a second look to see that. The more tightly sealed they were, the more goods there were on illuminated display between the front doors and sidewalk screens. It was security by smugness, the merchants showing off to foreigners what exactly it was good Danes would never stoop to steal. Madsen had been exactly wrong about the airport bank: Why *not* promote it as Tivoli since the whole culture was an amusement park!

Two army trucks crawling down the street erased the thought. The searchlights atop the cabs didn't miss a foot of wall or sidewalk on either side. Six soldiers in full battle gear sat in the open back of each vehicle. For all the sense of national trauma I had got from Madsen about the bank robbery, I had evidently still underestimated the local impact of what had occurred. For sure, only officials with pre-empted agendas would have still been counting on Army patrols rather than policemen for tracking down the thugs so long after the incident. Panic could be so counterproductive.

One of the searchlights hit me fully in the face. I caught myself before flinching. As the trucks moved on down Frederiksborggade, I leaned out to see if I had made an impression on one of the soldiers in the back. None looked up at me. For some reason, I thought of Salerno's older brother Giorgio dodging the Nazis and Fascists during World War II. The whole family had moved in on me!

I found a twenty-four-hour cafeteria across the street from the central train station. The half-hour walk in the mild night had restored my appetite, and I settled down at a window table with the equivalent of two meals at home, an enormous cheese salad and some kind of thinly sliced liver and onion concoction. Although only a quarter of its tables were occupied, the cafeteria seemed noisy, felt subtly energetic. Most of the customers were students divided by what appeared to be ethnic groups, Africans at one table, Spaniards at another, German being spoken at a third. I blamed Salerno's influence, his gabble about feeling like the eternal foreigner, for speculating how awkward it would be for me to go over and sit at any of the student tables. Why would I have wanted to sit at them in the first place?

I noticed the white-haired woman with the Irish Setter first. She was coming down Vesterbrogade, oblivious to the dog's pulls on the leash because she was fascinated by something happening down the street beyond my window. Then the two who looked like fishermen broke off their conversation at the edge of the sidewalk to match the woman's gaze. Across the avenue, other pedestrians were already looking in the same direction.

A thin, black woman in a tangerine dashiki came rushing in the door and over to the table of African students. Her high-pitched voice was enough to stop talk at nearby tables, and when words sounding like *airport* and *police* came out of her excitement, even an elderly Danish couple broke off from their gloomy staring competition to look out at the street. When I turned back outside, the woman with the dog and the fishermen were already gone and the people across the street were walking rapidly toward whatever had attracted them. I took it as a bad sign that even a Danish patrolman went trotting past my window.

Half the cafeteria was out the door before I put my liver on hold and gave in to my curiosity. Stepping out into the street was like entering a wind tunnel. All of Vesterbrogade seemed to be blowing down toward the Radhusplads, where hundreds of people had already gathered and scores of others seemed to be adding to the number from every direction. A teenager with a fringe blond haircut and an unnatural hop to his walk saw my hesitation as he passed. "The bank robbers!" he said, without breaking stride. "Swedes and Norwegians!"

I didn't know which presumption was more irritating, that I spoke English or that I would be as relieved as he was that the hunted killers weren't Danes. But he also made up my mind for me about my liver. I got there more deliberately than those rushing past me, but ended up in the same broad plaza with them. I've never been comfortable in crowds, and the mood of the one around me didn't convert me. There was too much silence for so many flushed faces and troubled eyes. The focus of attention was four patrol cars parked jaggedly off one another within a cordon of dozens of uniformed and plainclothes police. I made out a handcuffed prisoner in the back of one of the cars and assumed his accomplices were in the other vehicles. But what was everybody waiting for?

The three official-looking people, two men and a woman, standing in front of the Radhus's glass door told me: They were waiting for me. All the mes. They were all but counting the crowd on their fingers. Rather than being concerned by the swelling numbers in the plaza, the three of them looked like they were bringing some important calculation to term. Was one of them planning a speech? I lit a cigarette to blot out the possibility.

A state television van trundled across the square and came to a halt next to the patrol cars. Almost simultaneously, a second television truck, representing a Swedish network, came in from the opposite direction. The woman official, a long-necked brunette in a grey suit and heavy shoes immediately held up two fingers to a moustached plainclothesman who had been waiting for the signal; he in turn whispered something into the ear of the uniformed officer standing next to him.

I was furious as I watched the uniformed officer approach the driver of the nearest patrol car. I hadn't seen so much sensationalism outside the Olympic Games! The suspects couldn't have even signed statements yet, let alone have been processed, but a provocative spectacle was already under full mounting. And if the evidence against the suspects proved deficient, forcing them to be released somewhere down the road? Obvious: Only the police would be ridiculed for the premature triumphalism.

I started to turn away from the galling exhibition when the lights from the first television truck opened like a shell burst over the patrol cars. Deep guttural sounds rose from the neatly dressed man next to me, then something whimpering from the woman behind me. The eerie silence split apart by clumps all over the square. Mutterings, growlings, whole words popped out. The thought flashed through my mind that I didn't have to shoulder my way back out to the boulevard, that the crowd would simply dissolve into a clear path for me. But then the second light erupted out of the second-floor window of the Radhus, a spotlight so blinding it seemed to be scolding me for having regarded myself as merely some minor element in the scene. I felt the difference instantly: The light from the television truck was for illuminating the special interests of the reporter with her microphone, the light from the window was for entrapping everyone in the civic circus. When the Swedes turned on their truck lights from the other end of the square, it was superfluous: It hadn't occurred to me to escape in that direction, anyway.

I dared not move. The first two prisoners yanked from the patrol cars were far too likely in their callous appearance. The grumbled word *Svensk* was far too clear around me. Something metallic, some kind of rod, a screwdriver, clanked off the roof of one of the patrol cars. There was a heave of approval from people on the far right of the crowd, then whelps of disapproval, but the cordon guards seemed to look everywhere but there. I picked out a bald-headed officer who had too many studs and stripes for the dullness in his eyes, and started to raise my hand to indicate where he should have been looking. I realized, only at the last second, that would have made me as much of an imbecile as he looked: In his place, I certainly would have gone after the first raised arm I spotted.

The yelling and what I took to be cursing came more freely as the last of the five prisoners was hauled out of a car, straightened up between his escorts, and marched past the three politicians to the police building behind the Radhus. But aside from a rolled up newspaper, no more objects were thrown. The woman with the heavy shoes waited until the television cameramen had their last shots of the prisoners being taken off. Then she set her face grimly and walked over to the Danish television reporter with the microphone. Only in the light from the television truck did I recognize her: not the mayor of Copenhagen, but the prime minister of Denmark!

The national crisis appeared to be over.

And so I was back in the square alone with nobody at all sharing my anger about Mario Salerno.

Even in Madsen's car to the airport the next morning, I didn't know I wasn't returning directly to Paris. Why shouldn't I have been going home? I had heard all there was to hear from Denise Rosen. When, and if, the time came for putting her remarks on the record, Jens could take care of it. He had already seen to Johnny Stuck, getting in touch with Amsterdam to take a statement from *The Northern Sky* seaman and to keep an eye out for a possible visit from Salerno. There was nothing else for me to do *except* return to France and more prosaic affairs.

So why did the question even occur to me?

As usual, Madsen thought I was comical. "I can see it now," he said, raising his voice for the benefit of three scrawny cows out to pasture that we passed. "French Official Arrested in Square Riot! Bashes Two Cops Before Taken Into Custody!"

He had been in a frivolous mood since breakfast, and didn't care if I attributed it to his evening with Rosen, the capture of the bank robbers, or the next lunar eclipse. "That isn't what I said."

"No, what you said, Robert, was that the crowd helped you consider the virtues of being out of control. For your reasons, not theirs, but still out of control. And being the shrewd psychologist I am, I immediately land on that notion of *consider*. Robert Frenaud doesn't take a piss like the rest of us, he considers taking one!"

"Save your analyses for your suspects."

He brought his smile back to himself as he slowed down at the sight of a tie-up a mile ahead. "Do you hear it, Robert?"

"What?"

"The air, man! The great national sigh of relief! What else? Like that kid who ran past you last night. *We* never killed those people in the bank. *We* never caused a law and order crisis. It was *them,* the Swedes and Norwegians and Arabs and Chinese and all those others who have been exploiting our lax immigration laws. But worry about that later. Right now, let's get back to our phlegmatic superiority."

I thought of what Salerno had written about closing his mind within the borders where he happened to be living. Maybe he wasn't so uniquely artificial, after all.

"A small confession Robert. Your friend Salerno interests me for more reasons than doing you a favour."

"How else would you have met the buxom blonde?"

"From what you tell me, he might be the perfect sociopath."

"A what?"

He directed his rueful smile at the columns of crawling traffic. "My own term. The way I see them, sociopaths are individuals who, in the guise of proposing new ideas or urging new social models, really have only vindictiveness as a clear aim. They're people intent on avenging history, on punishing what they see as a process of evil at its roots."

"Don't tell me you've got lawyers up here taking that kind of defence for their clients."

"Not yet. But who knows?"

"So you've never actually met one of these sociopaths."

He didn't make his shrug look like a concession. "Take the United States in Europe just since World War II. They've done a lot of strong-arm things, Italy, Greece, Turkey, Belgium, just about everywhere. Sometimes there was a velvet glove to make us look less embarrassed about going along. Sometimes, like with Al-Qaeda, we've anticipated them, joined them willingly. But we've never been left in doubt about what kind of government, what kind of economy, what kind of social policies, would appeal to Washington and what kind wouldn't."

"It's called having power, Jens."

"Absolutely. But what we've never really looked into is how the reality of that power has seeped down into our societies. I'm not talking about the impact on our political parties, but on our individual psyches. The historical psychological impact."

"I didn't know there was such a thing."

"That's why you're privileged to know me."

"Good. The next time you come to Rouen, you can take my kids out for a walk past McDonald's and you can see first-hand how the power filters down into the psyche."

He nodded. "Agreed. One reaction. But I'm talking about the other side of it, the resentments this American power has bred on personal, intimate levels as much as on government or political ones."

"There will always be terrorists finding their excuses."

"But I'm not talking about terrorists, Robert. I'm talking about the resentments you find in law offices, medical studios, middle-of-the-road political parties, art galleries, bars, and boutiques. People just as resentful on an individual level as radical movements are, but not as organised to publicise or act upon their feelings."

"Good for all the police departments."

"And bad for the sociopath because he's doomed from the start. He'll never gain satisfaction because his target, the consequences and dynamics of history, is as abstract as his vindictiveness is compulsively concrete."

The sight of a KLM 737 rising up from the airport unnerved me. I liked planes parked on tarmac or hundreds of miles distant in the sky, not showing me their undercarriage. "At which point your sociopath, might settle for individual personifications of what he wants to eradicate. People, not history with a capital H."

Madsen looked delighted. "He might. But isn't it obvious even that solution wouldn't satisfy the kind of personality we're talking about? A personification remains that, Robert. It can never really match the hunger for vindicating history as such. How can it when our sociopath perceives history as merely a projection from his own tormented existence? As long as he continues living, so does his vendetta, and that means one futile personification after another. Hitler, for instance, was a classic case. After the Jews, he had the Gypsies and then the Slavs and so forth. There can never be any completion for that kind of disturbed individual."

"But Hitler had the Master Race rationalization."

"Meaning?"

"Meaning you're so much the psychologist, Jens, you can't see the wood for the trees. What might be incomplete on a psychological level isn't necessarily so politically or socially. For the Nazis the gratifications weren't just possible, they were ordained by policy. And rationalisations have a messy way of establishing their own standards of satisfaction."

Madsen was impressed, but not as much as I thought he should have been. "Okay. But note your example contains an element of authority. Hitler's rationalisations were supported by the German state. What about the sociopath who lacks patronage, whose rationalisations lack the sympathy of vested interests? A sociopath whose recourse to individual scapegoats exposes him to retribution as senselessly as his victims?"

"That's somebody in a very precarious position."

"Exactly!"

I was barely aware we had stopped before the Air France terminal. I thought of what Rosen had said about Salerno's doleful look on the bed after she had awoken. Then I thought again of the line from Salerno's book that had been waiting for me in my hotel room after I had been the one waking up. 'The artificial as part of the consolation'.

"What's that?"

"I'm not sure. But suppose our sociopath has another kind of authority stemming from the very transparency of his rationalisations?"

For once, Madsen looked stumped. "Like what?"

"Well, for instance, when we shave in the morning, we know we'll have to shave again the following morning. But that still doesn't stop us from thinking we've done a complete job as we put away the razor."

"You're referring to something specific, Robert. What?"

His look of anticipation was infuriating. How many times did he want to hear I didn't know? "When I figure it out, I'll call you. But it might have something to do with Keller and Salerno."

He tried not to look disappointed. "Figure it out, Robert," he smiled. "A new branch of psychological studies hangs in the balance."

It was too glib a farewell, and I wished I had more to bring into the terminal with me. Then I found myself again in front of the shuttered bank with three machinegun-toting guards. They were looking as vigilant as ever about protecting what had already been done. In fact, the last twenty-four hours had *all* been about what had already been done. Rosen had had her stories about *The Northern Sky* and her almost-lethal tryst with Salerno. The mob at the Radhusplads had had their glimpse of the arrested suspects. That wouldn't have satisfied Emile Josselin, I realised. As he had said, if I truly wanted to get Salerno, I should have got there ahead of his crime, not behind it.

The Air France woman behind the counter looked annoyed when I asked her about the possibilities for a stop-off in Amsterdam.

Johnny Stuck lived on a ladder. By the time I had negotiated the dark, steep staircase to the top floor of his building, bowling balls seemed to be weighing down my insteps.

The seaman was a shaggy-haired giant in his late forties or early fifties. As he pulled a T-shirt, with the likeness of Napoleon, down over his ample stomach, he waved me off the hall landing into the apartment with the air of having gone as far as he intended going with any representative of the French police. Inside was a kitchen smelling of oranges and coffee grounds, then a corridor with several mattresses piled against the wall, then a broad living room where chairs, tables, and an L-shaped couch had been buried under clothes, dirty glasses, and saucers filled with cigarette butts. Schubert murmured from a radio speaker between two windows facing onto the canal.

"What time is it?"

"Little after noon."

Stuck nodded as though he had expected worse and took a rumpled pack of cigarettes from his jeans pocket. A freckled redhead looking about sixteen, and wearing only a blue pyjama top, appeared out in the corridor, removed something from between the standing mattresses, then padded off again. The apartment was listed under Stuck's daughter, but I couldn't imagine even libertarian Holland signing leases with young teenagers.

"Keller a suicide, heh? Sad."

Sad. The tiny word rattled around the room. It was the first expression of genuine regret I had heard about George Keller's death.

"Was he drunk?"

"No sign of that, no."

He found a saucer to his liking in the clutter and dropped down on an ottoman. "You wouldn't tell me anyway. Cops never tell you a damn thing."

"Mr Stuck…"

"Everybody calls me Johnny Sticks."

"I thought you'd prefer your own name."

"That's what people know me as. That makes it mine."

"If you like."

"I like."

"In your statement to Sergeant Mulisch…"

"Another cop."

"You told Sergeant Mulisch you were the one who hired Keller for *The Northern Sky*."

"Then that's what I did."

"You're responsible for hiring crewmen for the ship?"

"I didn't say that."

What had I counted on, a quick five minutes of revelation? I cleared a bath towel and a pile of magazines from a chair and sat down. At least he didn't object. "The last I heard, *The Northern Sky* was somewhere in the Baltic. How come you're here?"

"A good ship," he said, looking more interested in the Schubert than in the question. "Captain Barfoed and I have an arrangement. He leaves me off in Rotterdam on the way north and picks me up again on his way back to the Atlantic. Good man Barfoed. I only lose a few dollars, I can spend my pay in Amsterdam instead of Riga, and I get to see my daughter." He caught my glance out to the hallway. "No, that's not her. That's Wabien, her friend. I thought you wanted to talk about Keller."

And Patricia Mariani, I thought. Neither of which had anything to do with Stuck's cradle robbing. "Go ahead. You were saying?"

He gave me the benefit of the doubt. "Captain's orders. We were a man short on the crossing and Barfoed never likes giving anything away to the company. He's a good man. So he tells Borg, that's the first officer, to go to the union hall in New York and get somebody. But Borg has plans for some actress and don't want to spend his time arguing with the union over insurance and tells Johnny to go to the hall. That night I find Keller."

"Just like that?"

"You want coffee? Johnny isn't awake yet. Wabien!"

The redhead appeared in the corridor again, this time in jeans and a grey pullover and looking closer to twenty than sixteen. Whatever her age, she didn't like being treated as a waitress. "My daughter, Joke, thinks I'm an old stuffed animal," Stuck laughed after Wabien had gone off again. "But Wabien tells her that's not true, Johnny is a pet. She thinks she can train me."

"You make it sound easy to find somebody for a ship."

His smile faded as fast as it had surfaced. "There's a bar down in Chinatown. The owner used to be on the ships and knows what you can get. The truck drivers come in and like to hear about the girls in Amsterdam. Keller was there trying to sell his passport."

I was saved from showing something stupid by a sudden banging of crockery out in the kitchen. Stuck winced for both of us. "The drivers in the bar, they go places in the south and sell the passports they buy in New York. Mexicans and Cubans, mainly. But Keller's passport says he's a painter, and you can't sell that because Immigration only has to stop one of these Mexicans and tell him to draw a picture..."

I had my own picture: of Blanc, Josselin, Rachel, even Jens Madsen sitting around a conference table and concluding that, yes, Robert Frenaud was a troubled soul to have travelled so far to be rewarded only with Johnny Stuck's ludicrous tales.

"...So Keller's telling me how easy it can be to sell his passport in Europe. Like Johnny Stuck don't know the business! So I tell him no thanks, because since I leave the ship at Rotterdam, your cop friends here think I'm selling something and are watching me all the time. They don't believe I get off because I like to see my daughter and Wabien, not all those crazy people in Riga. Fuck 'em is what

94

I say." He stabbed his dead butt into the saucer and immediately reached for another cigarette. "The owner tells Keller to leave me alone, Keller apologizes to me, so I buy him a beer."

"And that's when you hired him?"

He got up from the ottoman with a heavy laugh and pulled a plaid work shirt out of the heap of clothes on the couch. "No, I hired him after we almost got blown up!"

If he was testing me, I failed. "Blown up?"

He seemed satisfied with my expression. "Yeah. See, some of the drivers like to joke with Johnny. When they hear Keller needs money, they tell him about this truck that has to be driven to Philadelphia that night. There's something not right about it, but Keller don't care. The drivers give him the address of a warehouse on the West Side. He looks so happy! Then the drivers dare Johnny to go with Keller because I go to sea too much and don't know what truck tyres are. Jokes like that. Make everybody laugh. The people in the warehouse want two drivers and it's five hundred dollars each, so why not? Everybody cheers..."

A glass-enclosed tourist launch passed from one window to the other, and I wished I was aboard. At least then I could have told myself I was *officially* on vacation.

"...We go to the warehouse about three o'clock in the morning. Two of them are waiting. Dressed up like businessmen. There's a truck there all right, but who needs a truck for drugs? Then I wished it *was* just drugs!"

"What was it?"

"Two boxes of nitro-glycerine!"

"Stolen?"

"What the fuck difference does that make? I drive on a highway once or twice a year, and they want us to use side roads at night! I said to them, you crazy? No way."

"And Keller?"

"Keller says he'll take the money. Then one of the businessmen asks if he has a licence to drive a truck. He don't have *any* licence, not even for a car! I figure that's the end of it, but this second businessman says he don't care if the truck gets to Philadelphia. You know what happened then!"

"No, Johnny, I don't."

He shook his head at me in pity. "The two of them start arguing about how important the licence is! Johnny knows what that means. When you get the captain and the company agent arguing about how to do the job, they end up arguing about your pay, too. That's what I told Keller." He shook his head in dismay. "Maybe he should've gone in the truck, yeah? Then he don't kill himself... where did you say?"

"Rouen. So you talked him out of going."

"Wasn't me. Two other boys came along. They had licences. All we got was a wave goodbye. Keller was miserable. That's when I hired him."

He seemed finally out of tales. "Did you also hire a woman?"

He was mystified. "We only needed one hand... Oh, you mean Miss Kierkegaard, one of the passengers?"

"No, not Denise Rosen. What about a Patricia Mariani?"

"Who's that?"

Only one answer occurred to me: I didn't know. Wabien couldn't have picked a better moment to arrive with a tray holding a coffee pot, three mugs, cream, and sugar.

"Now everybody has to be quiet," Stuck said, pulling a cell phone out of another heap. "Johnny has to know when to be in Rotterdam. The radio says there's a storm, so maybe I get to stay here longer."

Wabien handed me a mug with a sceptical look as Stuck made his call; her soft, fawn-like features doubled the strength of her warning. She waited only for him to start bellowing at whoever answered to say: "You want to know the truth about this painter, yes? Then you should not believe about the passports and the explosives on the truck."

"He's been lying?"

She glanced over to where Stuck was tearing into the person at the other end of the line; there was affection in her expression, but it sat within some greater bemusement. "Johnny does not lie," she said lowly. "But sometimes he makes people think he does not know part of the truth. The story about the nitro-glycerine in the truck I heard from his daughter many years ago when we were at school. It happened. Joke's mother told her about it. But I don't think it happened with this painter. The passports I do not know. He always talks about this bar in New York. I am sure it exists. Did he meet this painter there? I do not know. This is important for you to know, yes?"

Stuck slammed down the receiver before I could thank her. "They fuck up the dates for Rotterdam! Now I have to go down to the office and call Barfoed directly!"

"I told him maybe you were exaggerating, Johnny."

What planet were the two of them born on? His only response was a dismissive wave before he started filling his pockets with a lighter, pens, and other junk. "Tell him what you want."

"That's not being helpful, Johnny," I finally found the voice to say. "I came here at great effort because I thought you could help."

"They pay your fare. All official business to you."

"That's not the point," she said icily. "This man is dead. Maybe he left behind people who would like to know why."

"Okay, okay!" And with that, he marched over to a CD cabinet in the corner of the room, hefted out a grey duffel bag behind it, and shook the bag's contents out over the floor. "This is everything Keller gave me to hold," he said defiantly.

I had to play back the announcement to myself before daring to believe it. "This stuff belongs to Keller?"

He laughed; hollowly. "Not anymore."

On the floor were a pair of worn brown corduroys, a brown woollen sweater, a paperback of Kokoschka drawings, and a pocket English-Italian dictionary. I had no more doubts about George Keller's ultimate destination.

Stuck was watching me intently. "Not too much you're thinking?"

I crouched down to the items mainly to get away from the man's stare. I saw a hard square in the back pocket of the corduroys and removed it. It was an address book with a red cover, a twin to the one Keller had left behind at the Hotel Flamant. But the contents weren't at all the same. Unlike the book in Rouen, this one's every page was clogged with names, addresses, phone numbers, crossed out names, crossed out addresses, and crossed out phone numbers. There seemed to be no pattern at all. There were script entries and block letters, numerous ink colours, at least three or four different hands. It was such a mess, such an attack on my theories about address books, that I almost missed the MARIANI 787-9556 on a *P* page.

"That's the woman you said," Stuck said over my shoulder.

"And you never met her?"

"No. Why should I? Give it to me."

I ignored his hand. "Sorry. It's evidence."

"For what?"

"For an investigation we're conducting in cooperation with the Dutch authorities. I have no official standing to confiscate this here and now, but I can make a call and you'll still have to surrender it."

He thought I was funny, and looked over to Wabien to see if she thought so, too. "It's not yours, Johnny," she said evenly.

"It's more mine than his! Keller gave it to me!"

"You mean he just left all this stuff behind at Le Havre, don't you?"

"Yeah? So? That against the law in France?"

"Why did you take it?"

"You're a cop. You wouldn't understand."

"Tell him why, Johnny."

He looked so shame-faced in front of her I knew there was at least one thing he hadn't lied about: The hulk *was* her tamed bear. "I tell myself in Le Havre maybe one day Keller finishes all his drinking and punching people and remembers what he left behind on the ship. So he calls up the company office and they tell him Johnny Sticks has it."

"But now that he's dead?"

He gave a light kick to the corduroys. "I think about bringing the stuff back to New York, calling up people in that book, and asking if they want it. They don't, no problem. I'll throw everything in the garbage. But at least it'll be garbage in a place Keller knew, not in some goddam Rouen."

"You should give everything to the woman the gentleman has been talking about," Wabien said behind a sip of coffee.

He nodded. "Yeah, maybe to her. Where is she, Frenchy?"

"I was hoping you could tell me."

He reached down abruptly and scooped the sweater, pants and books back into the duffel bag. "You hoped wrong."

Watching him re-gather the last possessions of George Keller, I was tempted to toss the address book back into the pile: After all, he couldn't very well offer the old pants to somebody in New York whose number he didn't have. But I couldn't afford that kind of sentimentality, not with the evidence in my hand that Patricia Mariani had indeed been responsible for bringing George Keller together with Mario Salerno. Keller's pants and sweater were just going to have to end up in an Amsterdam garbage can.

I waited until we were walking to Stuck's tram, at the Muntplein, to get the answer Denise Rosen had been unable to give me. Away from Wabien's quietly critical gaze, he practically swashbuckled his way through the crowded lunch hour sidewalks. "Where was he going? He was going to Norway. That's where the ship was going."

"But when you talked together, he never mentioned heading for some place after that?"

"Like where, Frenchy?"

"Italy, for instance."

He stopped to gape exaggeratedly at two blondes in short skirts, and to be appreciated for his mugging by a passing cyclist. And I realized his answer didn't matter. None of it had been about George Keller's plans for Italy, it occurred to me; it had all been about Patti Mariani's destination in Europe. Johnny Sticks's artificiality was the consolation.

I returned home to suspended judgments. Blanc hadn't liked hearing about my extra hop to Amsterdam from third parties but was mollified enough by my offer to pay for it personally that he tut-tutted "We take it one step at a time." Translation: If visiting Johnny Stuck proved to be instrumental in establishing a crime and Mario Salerno as its perpetrator, the additional airfare would be assigned to the Sûreté's ledgers. By making this prospect sound like a certainty, I also got Rachel to hold off from all but the most formal of reminders that we were hardly in a position to 'advance money' to my office. I couldn't have agreed more, and suggested we make up for it by adding a simple pasta to the weekly dinner schedule. Her look said that was overkill, but, like Blanc, left the idea for further developments.

My staff had weathered my absence without trauma. Beneath her bright greeting, Odile even seemed dejected the noisemakers and party hats would have to be returned to the closet. Josselin, of course, showed nothing. There had been progress on this, not too much progress on that. Of course, his grocery list left out anything to do with Salerno. "You still haven't tracked down Mariani, I gather," I said, capitulating.

"Milan."

"Excuse me?"

He showed nothing as he found a printout in his jacket pocket and handed it to me. "Alitalia. New York to Milan. July 8."

"What took so long to find this?"

He raised his eyebrows in resignation to the ways of the non-Breton world. "The nearest thing I got to an answer was they did their first search for a Marianni, two *n*'s. I checked with Milan. They have no hotel or other record of her."

"Rome? She might have gone directly south."

"Checked that, too. No Mariani anywhere in Rome. I wasn't expecting to find her there anyway."

"Why not?"

He sighed indulgently. "If she wanted to go to Rome, why not just fly there from New York instead of going to Milan first?"

"Maybe because…"

"No, I already checked that. There were no Alitalia flights from New York to Rome that week that were fully booked. Not even close. There was no reason not to go there directly if that's where she intended going."

I thought I got the drift. Having failed to talk me out of my obsession, Josselin was determined to brandish his zeal as the ultimate argument for proving I was going nowhere. "So you think she was…?"

"Could be anywhere," he shrugged. "She doesn't sound like a stranger to picking up people. She meets somebody on the plane to Milan, they land and go off to Switzerland, Austria, or the Sudanese refugee camps because that'll be such a great adventure."

"Or maybe…"

"Or maybe," he said briskly, "because she bought a ticket to Milan, there was somebody specific she was going to meet there. And maybe this somebody took her to Switzerland, Austria, or the Sudanese refugee camps. And no, it wasn't Salerno. Between July 8 and July 11, he was chairing a conference in Rome. Something about the displaced people of Europe. No way he was the one who met her in Milan."

I fell back on my calm. The scrupulous Josselin appeared to have cut off all accesses. But I still resisted throwing my Out tray at him. I knew he had overlooked something more surely than I had ever known anything. "What about this Webber in Rome? The other name in the book?"

"So far nothing. He's probably some transient already gone."

It had sounded more persuasive coming from me than from him. "But we'll assume he's not, Emile. We'll assume he gets his mail at the post office because he lives in the place."

He nodded obediently. "And beyond that?"

"The logical. Work your way up and out from the northern frontier cities, west to east. Any hotel where Mariani, with or without a friend, might have stayed on the evenings of July 9 and July 10. And if that gets you nowhere, start with the trailer camps."

Josselin bolted in exasperation before I got around to tents and train station benches. Feeling proud of myself, I went through the stack of phone messages Odile had not been able to take care of, or reroute elsewhere, in my absence. Hellman from *Le Quotidien* wanted to put me on record about the rise in the muggings of foreign seamen. My old schoolmate, Alain Cleves, had called to remind me of our biannual luncheon, a ritual I had been finding increasingly awkward because of his puppy-dog probings about what social barriers the Frenauds had scaled since our previous get-together. The Gallant Club wanted to know if I could attend its next session to reassure its elderly membership that the Sûreté was not bending over backwards to defend the rights of immigrants at the expense of French citizens. Somebody named Simon FALANGE (!), as Odile put it, insisted on a meeting so he could persuade me of his son's qualifications for joining Special Affairs. Roger had called in case I had returned directly to the office from Copenhagen. And what had *that* been about? Neither he nor Rachel had mentioned any new crisis he might have preferred explaining to me before his mother.

I was about to call home then and there when I noticed that the last message was from Margaret Tierney. Immediately, I quickened at the thought that she had recalled something else pertinent from her indirect ties to Salerno in New York. I was already being passed to her by the American Consulate switchboard operator when it occurred to me there was nothing else pertinent she could have possibly remembered, that I had advanced well beyond Salerno's street protest days.

"All these mysterious trips," Margaret cooed. "Your secretary made it sound like you were touring secret bunkers at the front."

"Why she's my secretary. How can I help you, Margaret?"

"Actually, maybe I can help you, and throw in a meal at the same time. Jean and I are having a dinner party Friday in honour of an old friend who's visiting. Guess who?"

I almost blurted Salerno's name before remembering she had apparently never known the man.

"The woman we were discussing, my old roommate Jill Faber. She's a travel writer now and she's here for a few days. I thought there was a little synchronicity in that, so why don't you and Rachel come and meet her? She can tell you a lot more about Salerno than I can."

"Actually, Margaret, Salerno isn't really…"

"Oh, c'mon. It'll be a chance for Rachel to escape the kitchen."

"You sound like a hostess afraid of having empty places at the table."

"Then you'll come?"

"How could I possibly abet a social embarrassment?"

My oafishness felt like a ribbon on the morning. Dourness hung up my phone. What gave Margaret Tierney the right to talk about Rachel as though they had been lifelong confidantes when in fact they hadn't seen one another in years, and even then at some crowded reception or other? And what was to be gained talking to some travel writer who had probably reduced entire civilizations to continental breakfasts? I didn't want to go to any damn dinner at the LaSalle house.

Rachel couldn't have been more delighted with the invitation and with my response to it. At dinner, she openly humoured my questions about the summer school companion Roger had been given permission to eat with. She seemed to have one long wink for Janine through my stuttering explanation of the difference between the fairy tales written by Hans Christian Andersen and the Grimm brothers. In the living room after supper, with the dishwasher rattling from the kitchen and her moisturizer smelling more like medicine than soap, she couldn't have been gayer about the clothes choices awaiting her. Would her white sleeveless turtleneck and jeans be okay or would that have been a gaffe with high-echelon attorneys? What about her silver lamé suit and matching pumps? How formal was a dinner at the LaSalle house, anyway? Maybe she should drop around to Arlene's boutique and buy that cocktail dress that cost the equivalent of almost two weeks of my salary, would I recommend she do that?

"You're having a good time, I hope."

She smiled slyly at the liquid she rubbed over the back of her hand. "Absolutely. And we haven't even got there yet, *cheri!*"

Why be only irritable when a little effort could make it worse? "I thought you were bored by official people. Isn't that what you told me coming home from the Marton's that night?"

She found an unwanted speck on a knuckle; it was me. "That was about a year ago, Robert. I didn't realise saying that would condemn me to being seen in society only with members of my family or yours." She capped the moisturizer bottle, got up from the couch, and marched off with enough stateliness for the Champs d'Èlysée. "Thank god you've got this obsession with your Italian radical friend. Cultivate it, Robert. It seems to be good for our social calendar."

The LaSalles lived in a dowdy building a stone's throw from the Flaubert House. If I hadn't already been there many years before, I would have taken one look at the scarred slate walls of the foyer and one whiff of the neighbourhood cats and instantly walked back out into the street in search of more appropriate accommodation for one of the most celebrated legal minds of the province. But thanks to my previous experience, I went right past a stone staircase (which curved up only so far as a brick wall halfway to the second floor) and over to a modest gate in the rear of the foyer. Rachel kept her nose crinkled against the cat stink as I used the intercom on the gate to call upstairs and announced myself to somebody who sounded like hired help. She still wasn't convinced of our destination even after a buzzer opened the gate and I led her to a shabby blue door that was an elevator.

"It looks like a broom closet!"

"Deception is at the heart of security."

As she took in the car's beige carpeting and faux candelabrum with a snort, I had an urge to kiss her. "Let's have fun, Rachel."

It sounded novel coming out of my mouth, so why shouldn't it have surprised her, too? As the car creaked its way up to the top of the three-floor building, I told myself there had been months of better times and better places for clasping her hand and feeling part of something more than my job. The trouble was, I couldn't say what they were.

The door opened on the kind of crowd scene I thought I had left behind in Copenhagen. There was a sea of hands to be shaken, in a couple of cases even of people I knew. Margaret wore the same kind of pants suit Rachel had chosen, only in tan instead of green. Jean LaSalle looked paunchier from the last time I had seen him on television, but was tall enough and had enough grey flecking his hair to strike the figure of the urbane host long accustomed to handling the last-minute social obligations thrust on him. There were semi-familiar faces from the American community and the magistrature. There were two waiters circulating with hors d'oeuvres and a third one manning a table bar. There was the cause of my next consternation, even Blanc.

"I think I've been invited to keep you on a leash," he smiled as he took Rachel's hand. "Margaret is afraid you'll whisk her guest of honour away to an interrogation room."

Was I imagining Margaret's air of satisfaction peering over at us from the other side of the room? I didn't think so. And the message seemed to be that even minor consulate officials couldn't afford to have all their eggs in one Sûreté basket. "The idea has its appeal."

Blanc laughed dutifully; Rachel knew me better and didn't. Since neither Margaret nor LaSalle had thought to introduce me, I picked out Jill Faber on my own. She was in a corner trying to look interested in what Bochy from Licences was saying to her. She was a severely thin brunette in her early fifties with close-cropped hair, tired eyes, and the tiniest of hands around her wine glass. She looked nothing at all like Denise Rosen or, I was confident to imagine by now, Patricia Mariani. Salerno's catholic tastes grew more irritating with every past lover I came across.

Bochy withdrew to the bar for a refill, and I immediately left Rachel to Blanc. I was already halfway across the room, committed to my target, when I realised I should have emulated Bochy and got a drink of my own. "I believe we have a mutual acquaintance," I said, hoping that lighting a cigarette would make me look more nonchalant.

Jill Faber sighed without apology, apparently before the one scheduled part of the evening she could have done without. "If the past and present are mutual acquaintances. What's he up to these days?"

"I don't really know. His name came up…"

"Margaret said. He's involved in some case of yours?"

"That's still open to question, how involved he is."

She flagged down one of the waiters with a raspy laugh. "Listen to us!" she said, grabbing a celery stalk without a napkin. "Talking about this great hovering presence! *He* this, *he* that. Do we get hit by lightning if we actually say his name?"

"Salerno."

"No, we have to say it fully three times to exorcise it. Mario Salerno. Mario Salerno. Mario Salerno."

"You feel the need to exorcise him after so long?"

It sounded official even to me, so I rushed on while she took a more considered look at her celery. "Margaret has told me some things and they may be everything there is to know. I haven't the slightest idea if you can tell me anything else."

She gave me a passing mark. "Are you a person of compartments? Do you divide your fish and your fries and peas on the plate?"

"I'm sure Margaret's accused me of it."

"Oh, she accuses everyone. But I mean manic compartmentalisation. Hey, don't you want a drink or something? You're making me think you really have come only to interrogate me." She was already moving toward the bar. "What do I call you, by the way? Inspector? Monsieur Frenaud?"

"Robert is fine."

"Actually, it's imperative. I think it's so silly when people dance around calling each other something because they don't want to define what kind of relationship they're supposed to have."

"Maybe you're in those situations more than I am."

It hadn't really been a question, so she didn't have to acknowledge my answer. There were travails in being a travel writer outsiders couldn't understand. On the one hand, she had always regarded herself as a spontaneous, informal person. On the other hand, she had come across more than her share of hotel managers, restaurant owners, and tour operators who expected the most antiquated formalities in return for her free stays and fares. She didn't mean just Asians, either, where you might have expected stuffed shirts who had attended the Harvard Business School and who wanted to be thought of as King Louis XIV back home in Djakarta or Kuala Lumpur. Where she had really been brought up short had been in places like Italy and Russia. "They give you a hotel room in some gloomy dump in Moscow that was probably last used for a drug deal. You're the one who's going to publicise them, but they act like you should be grateful for having been received by the Czar. Use the wrong form of the verb in some of these places and it's like you've stolen the crown jewels…"

She went on, stoking up all my prejudices. And not just because she talked like another American for whom the rest of the world was merely a tourist map to be followed from one accommodating host to another. What teased me even more (with the help of my first scotch) was the thought that Jill Faber, impatient with the deficiencies of the international service industries, had once been idealistic enough about something to have risked arrest with Mario Salerno in New York. *The corruption was so satisfying!*

Too satisfying. "Why do I get the feeling you're entertaining me?"

She seemed to will her jaded stare to stay the course, to wait out my scepticism. But then the lamp behind my shoulder caught her eyes, and she released her guard. "Margaret said you're a man of many preconceptions."

"True or not, why play into them?"

She had heard it before, and was still hurt by it. "A character flaw. First noticed by somebody named Mario."

"And when did you first notice his?"

"I'd really like to know why you're interested, Robert."

The truth had never sounded so much like a lie. "There was a suicide here recently. An American painter. Salerno's name was in his address book. He was curious enough about it to come here."

"Is that a crime?"

"I didn't say it was."

"Mario's never been short on curiosity. Used to scold me I didn't have enough. Said I should develop a greater interest in the world. I don't think he had travel writing in mind, but…"

"Why you still need the exorcism."

She smiled; uncomfortably. "Well, it was real hard getting the CIA to conform to my ideas about where to go and what to do there, so writing for magazines seemed like the next best thing. And you're immediately thinking his approval shouldn't still be so important to me. And my answer to that is it's my approval that matters. That's what I picked up from him."

"To change the world?"

"You like it the way it is?"

"I don't think people like cousin Patti make it any better."

She laughed. "Nice. What do you want to know about her?"

Margaret postponed the thought by appearing from the back of the house with her teenaged son. He clearly preferred his bedroom to the aggressive way she introduced him around, extolling his schoolwork and guitar playing. I didn't need to catch Rachel's darts to understand that Mars would have landed on Rouen before she ever stooped to such a display with Roger. The second thought behind her stare? *"Well, how different is she from you, Robert? You're parading our children around like long-range social investments too, aren't you?"* Jill Faber went off to talk to somebody else, and I drank off Rachel's ludicrous comparison with another scotch.

There were too many guests for a sit-down meal, so the aircraft carrier of a teak dining table served as the buffet centre. The beef prompted thoughts of English cow disease, the snapper reminders of the last mercury reports I had seen before going to Denmark, and the greens impatience with the slowness of Brunel's investigation into some of the sprays being used on imported produce at the port markets. I ate off my lap, not as adroitly as Jill Faber and two members of Tierney's staff, but more ably than Blanc, who groused loud enough about the heat of the plate on his knees to win Margaret's pity and gain a specially cleared place for himself at a side table. When LaSalle joined him for what looked like a considered exchange on October's National Assembly elections, I was left to fret I had done too much of a good job separating my salmon from the asparagus and both from the whipped potatoes. I resolved that crisis by pushing the fish into the potatoes.

With dessert looming, I realised it was time to check in with Rolin at the office. I couldn't find Rachel and her cell phone, so went out to the kitchen where Margaret was appraising a chocolate cake she was about to serve. "What do you think, Robert?"

"Looks delicious. Is there a phone I can use?"

"In the bedroom if you want quiet. But I wasn't asking about the cake. What do you think of Jill?"

"She seems competent at what she does."

"*Competent?*"

"I've talked to the woman for five minutes, Margaret, and she's been avoiding me ever since. Down the hall to the bedroom?"

"Second door to the right. But don't think you're getting off with just *competent*."

The bedroom door was open, and so was the balcony door. Rachel and Jill Faber were standing outside. Even my dismay felt insufficient. Rachel's attentiveness to the American, slumped against the balcony wall, seemed almost protective. They were conversing so easily in English that Rachel, not Margaret Tierney, might have been Faber's one-time roommate in New York. The name Salerno wafted in from the harbour lights not once, but twice. And after all the scenes she had made over Roger's troubles in school, Rachel was posing boldly with a cigarette in her hand!

Faber laughed. "Caught us!"

Rachel seemed to consider discarding the cigarette, then just stared at me defiantly. "We were talking about your Italian friend."

"I don't have any Italian friends."

"Your wife asked about him, so I ended up telling her. You can get it from her now. Or do I have to say it all over again?"

I was petrified with anger. And even as I told myself it should have been about Salerno and Faber's blasé attitude, I thought of the afternoon at the Rue Corneille *tabac* when, wearing a maternity dress for the first time, Rachel had shaken her head to the cigarettes I had ordered for her and announced with absolute finality she was giving up smoking.

"You better, Jill, or the inspector will think I'm interfering in his internal affairs." She calmly jammed her cigarette into the balcony ledge, made sure it was out, then stepped back into the bedroom with the dead butt in her palm. "Something I don't want to be accused of."

I watched her all the way to the door. Eye contact would have been enough, but there was none, let alone some look of shame. She simply walked out, awkward enough not to be slinking, but not all that far from it, either.

"The gist of it is cousin Patti was everybody's excuse." It took me a moment to refocus on Faber. She was standing in the balcony doorway, her eyes running over the LaSalle bedroom as if committing its details to memory. "Salerno's excuse because he didn't have to stay faithful to anybody as long as he could look forward to her walking in the door any minute and dragging him away for her latest epiphany. Mine because I could blame her for breaking up my great romance with the dashing professor. And, God knows, an excuse for the powers-that-be because how could anybody take Salerno seriously about the important things when he played a part in her antics? Patti gave everybody a crutch."

It dawned on me what she had been taking in, not the LaSalle bedroom, but all the hotel rooms from Dublin to Beijing in which she had unpacked. "And ever since you've felt like the world's guest?"

Even in the dim light offered by the bed table lamp her eyes glinted. "Margaret warned me you were a prick."

"She flatters everybody, remember? So how have we all been wrong, judging Salerno by his cousin?"

She contemplated the door to the hallway, heard nothing reassuring in a burst of laughter from the living room, then stepped over to Margaret's vanity. "Because he could compartmentalise, that's how. When he was with Patti, he was with Patti. None of their clown shows affected what he did away from her, in his own head anyway. And when she wasn't around and he was fighting for something he really believed in, he never looked all that distraught. Clean cuts."

"You're so sure of this?"

"Years sure, Robert, Inspector, Monsieur. What it really meant was that in the end *I* wasn't something he believed in all that deeply. Me, he *didn't* compartmentalise. I was at the end of a lot of tables when she was around. Even when there were just the three of us, it felt like the end of the table. Why couldn't he have left me out of it altogether?"

"Maybe he wanted to impress her with you."

She was so small she didn't even rise to the top of Margaret's low mirror. "That's very gallant of you. And I guess I tried talking myself into it a couple of times. But Patti wasn't impressed by anybody. You could say the same thing to her three times in an hour, and she'd act every time like she hadn't heard it before. It was always what was going on in *her* head, what new enthusiasm had swept *her* up. Mario knew the ground rules. He didn't try to impress her with me or anybody else. It was all about her."

"Nothing I've heard about the man strikes me as that passive."

She traced a fingernail over the back of one of Margaret's brushes as though intimidated about picking it up. "Because you haven't seen him in action with Patti. He was always on eggshells with her around. He couldn't say anything accurately enough." She had enough of Margaret Tierney's brushes and combs. "Any more questions, Inspector?"

Only one occurred to me. "Would it surprise you after all this time that Salerno has become a violent man?"

"Doing what?"

"Whatever violence is capable of."

"We're talking about a lifetime since I've seen him. How the hell would I know?"

"Of course."

"You think he's done something. What?"

"Let's just say we have somebody missing and we have Salerno expending too much effort on denying he was with her recently."

I blamed the scotch, I credited the coffee. Whatever I had been drinking, it had got me to blurt out what seemed to have been rolling around in the back of my head for days.

"Patti?"

"Just speculation at this point."

She folded her arms around her and looked out at the balcony door. She savoured something, then it was gone. By the time she turned back, she had chosen me as the enemy. "You're not just a cop, are you? You're political. All these years and he still gets under the skin of people like you! Wow! Who would have imagined!"

"This has nothing to do with politics."

But she was past giving me the benefit of the doubt. "Then what? Your private speculation? I don't think so." She started for the door. "I wouldn't have thought it possible, but I'll still take his word over yours."

"Is he or isn't he capable of violence, Ms Faber?"

There was far too much of Rachel in her look: some profound pity she was ready to grant if I ever managed to get to the remote place where she was waiting. "Against himself. But I'm sure you know that."

"I'm talking about against others."

She shook her head. "You'd never make a good travel writer, Robert. When you make up things, people are going to show up expecting to find them. Won't do much for your reputation in the long run. Goodnight."

I thought about covering Margaret's bedroom floor with banana peels and running across them until I could fly over the balcony wall out into the harbour. It was in that mood that I listened to Rolin's monotonous recitation. The man had never had a sense of proportion, reporting fifty-euro robberies with the same emphasis as a port collision with casualties, and should have never been entrusted with the night desk. I liked thinking that the renewed laughter from the living room was about him, not because Jill Faber was relaying her bedroom conversation with Inspector Frenaud.

"...Mulisch says the Kroebbe woman didn't invite him in, kept him out on the landing..."

"What? What are you saying? Start that over again."

Rolin sighed. "Sergeant Mulisch in Amsterdam. He called to say Mario Salerno... That the name?"

"Go on, go on."

"This Mario Salerno visited a seaman under surveillance at the request of... I don't see what this has..."

"Madsen in Copenhagen. Get it out, Rolin."

There was a crinkling of paper in my ear. "The witness under surveillance was not at home. This Salerno spoke with a Wabien Kroebbe, who told him the witness had left that morning for Rotterdam. Salerno asked when he would be back. He left as soon as the Kroebbe woman told him the witness was sailing to New York from Rotterdam. I think that's the gist of it, Inspector. I don't see what Copenhagen..."

"You're doing fine, Rolin. What else?"

"Nothing really. This Kroebbe woman immediately called Mulisch after Salerno left. She had apparently been told to do that by the witness in case Salerno showed up..."

My first achievement on the evening: Johnny Stuck didn't hate cops enough to endanger Wabien.

"...Mulisch is faxing a full report, but it hasn't come in yet. Then there's another thing from Borgomanero, in Italy. An unidentified woman's body was found by the side of the highway. The report says she was shot once in the head."

I didn't dare hope. "Near Milan?"

"Borgomanero? It doesn't say."

"You have an atlas, man. Look it up."

With Rolin's throat too far away, my hands had to settle for lighting a cigarette. Rachel had been considerate of the LaSalles and their bedroom by smoking out on the balcony, but being considerate didn't seem like my responsibility. If the body in Borgomanero was Patricia Mariani, I was the one who had the apologies coming.

"Not too far from Milan," Rolin finally came back. "Going northwest toward the Swiss border."

"Tell me about the body."

He did, and it wasn't time yet to be filling the LaSalles' bedroom with smoke. The Italians were presuming the dead woman was an American because she had American labels on her clothes, but they had found no passport or other documents. They couldn't fix her age any more specifically than 'probably in her fifties' and they had no idea yet how she had ended up alongside a highway, killed there, pushed out after being shot in a car, or killed elsewhere and dumped on the scene. Officially, then, it could have been either Patricia Mariani or some Lithuanian who had stopped off in Italy on her way home from a shopping trip in New York.

It wasn't much to hang my hopes on, but at least it gave me something else to think about on the way home waiting for Rachel to explain herself. She was in no hurry. Their foibles, charms, and mysteries, she had an opinion of every one of the dinner guests. The only one she didn't have an opinion about was me. I was supposed to have one about her first, and until then I was just her driver.

"All right," I said finally, around the corner from the house. "I just don't like you sneaking around like an addict."

"I had one cigarette."

"Tonight."

"At least it got your attention."

"Jump in the Seine and I'll really pay attention."

"Probably. That would be official business."

And so on. It was not the way the evening was supposed to have ended. Maybe once upon a time I would have been seduced by her claim to making her self-righteousness equal to mine. Maybe once upon a time she would have found my appalled reactions to her behaviour erotic in the extreme. But as I let her out of the car in front of the house before going on to the garage, I wondered only why she had dithered so melodramatically for so long before finally selecting her pants suit. Whatever she had chosen, she would have been the same Rachel Fanon inside it, wouldn't she?

The next day brought little more information from Amsterdam or Borgomanero. Mulisch's fax merely recapitulated what Rolin had relayed to me, plus the one detail that Salerno had returned immediately to Rome after his visit to Wabien. The Italian police were able to say the dead woman had been shot somewhere else than where her body had been found, that the shooting had taken place a good two weeks before the discovery of the corpse, and that dental evidence also pointed across the Atlantic. Missing persons cases were being crosschecked and foreign companies operating in Milan and neighbouring cities had been asked to make sure no employee was unaccounted for.

I wasn't discouraged; on the contrary, Salerno's trip to Amsterdam after Johnny Stuck had given even Josselin and Odile pause. If we weren't talking about a panic to cover up something, what the hell were we talking about? The question seemed so obvious I spared Josselin the actual words. In turn, he spent the morning pressing the Italians for more word on Leo Webber's possible whereabouts.

Then Arnaud slipped into my office. His resignation hadn't affected his mousy movements: He still acted too anxious to please. He began talking about a European conference on contraband that was scheduled to open in Naples within three days. Two words into his spiel and my thoughts drifted to his wife, a drab, overweight woman (Claire?) who nevertheless had the cachet of a father who operated the largest or second largest private security company in the country. The wife, I thought, had probably knitted one dissatisfaction to another to produce a semblance of satisfaction for everybody. Her father would have preferred somebody a little more imaginative and less obsequious than Arnaud, but Arnaud had taken his daughter off his hands. For his part, Arnaud undoubtedly entertained fantasies more enthralling than his wife, but, mole that he was, he had burrowed into the indebtedness of his father-in-law. Try as hard as I did, I couldn't see the relevance of any of this to me and Rachel.

"...So I just don't think under the circumstances it would be proper, Inspector."

"What wouldn't?"

He gave me an odd look. "To go to Naples. You assigned me to the conference, and I'm grateful for your confidence. But I'll be leaving the Sûreté, and I don't think it would be in the section's best interests to send me. What would it look like if I make contacts down there and then they call to hear I no longer work in Special Affairs?"

Invulnerable logic, of course, and I probably should have been grateful to have an assistant who worried so much about the problems he might have been creating for co-workers he was about to leave behind. But once Arnaud had stolen off again, I was mainly left with the problem of finding somebody to send to Naples in his place. I couldn't afford the absence of Josselin or Brunel, and Blanc would have had a haemorrhage if I dispatched one of the junior members of the staff. What it came down to, in fact, was another comforting omen.

The trick to winning over a superior to an idea is to make him think it's been at least partly his own. Even if he sees through the tactic, he will appreciate an astute presentation that minimises his own commitment in case of failure and promises him full credit for success. But then there was Blanc, who sat rock-still behind his spindly-legged desk, staring and staring while I stumbled on. The man clearly had doubts about being associated with anybody named Frenaud.

When I ran out of words, he glanced down at the forearms he had braced against the rim of his desk, saw nothing untoward about their position, and cleared his throat. "Quite a bee you have circling around you, Robert," he said. "But if we humour it, does it give us honey or a sting in the eye?"

"I think it's already stung one person."

"Yes, yes. But even if that's true, we have what? A crime of violence committed on Italian territory by an Italian national? Or have you left out the part where this dead woman on the road took out French citizenship?"

"This all started…"

He lifted his arm dismissively and swivelled his leather chair directly around into the sunlight being funnelled in through his high window. The way he sat erect, stomach in, immaculate creases on his pants, reminded me of a mannequin. "I already know more than I want to know about this painter. And the Americans seem to feel the same way."

"I agree we've exhausted Keller. He was an unwitting player in what followed his death."

"Quite. And what is it *we* are being unwitting about?"

"Commissioner?"

"Come, come, Robert. Your personal agenda here. A dislike of the man's politics? Some envy of his love life? I smell the accusation of irresponsibility, but I need it located more specifically."

Blanc's deliberate profile made me think of Father Plesac from my school days; the more the old priest had wanted me to admit something, the more he had kept his eyes trained elsewhere. "Obviously, we wouldn't be the primary investigators in anything that occurred in Italy. But I believe we've developed significant evidence..."

"To turn it over to the Italians?"

"Yes."

He hadn't expected that answer. "Yes, you say?"

"We would have no grounds for objecting. That I know, Salerno has committed no crime here."

"Or possibly anywhere."

It was Plesac again: weighing the merits of my contrition, not wanting to hear evasions. "Always possible, but my intuition says otherwise."

He considered the word *intuition* aloud, but not all that sarcastically. Then he stood up, so carefully he might have been testing a cranky joint. "You know how I feel about you, Robert," he said, eyes on the floor. "I will not be behind this desk forever, and you're as qualified as anyone to succeed me. But once you walk into this office, your qualities as an investigator become secondary to your administrative abilities. You don't get bogged down in leads or clues, you accept or don't accept the leads and clues others bring you. You don't pit yourself directly against criminals, you make sure they and all the disorder they represent are on the far side of the shield put in place by your staff. The who and what are always important, but they must share priorities with the when." He came back up to me still frowning, but without the sunlight there as an excuse. "Do you understand me, Robert?"

It didn't even feel like me, *that* Robert Frenaud, who moved so presumptuously around the high-backed visitor's chair and, with Blanc still standing, perched down on it. So why did I let that creature out of my pocket? In retrospect, maybe because he was a judge. And just as I had sometimes been comforted by the presence of Father Plesac on the worm-eaten pew in the vestibule of Sacré Coeur where the old man had insisted on hearing confessions, it suddenly seemed all right for Blanc to be the one to mediate between me and a dozen separate good reasons that had come together to form a suspect impulse. How could he have possibly worried about decorum instead of the central issue?

"When I was younger, Commissioner, I used to think the worst sin in the world was lack of ambition. People who let themselves drift along from one day, one position, one responsibility to the next. Most of them would have denied vehemently they were passive creatures, would have recited their list of achievements for you, but that didn't change the fact they were essentially without ambition. Just because they acquitted a responsibility today didn't mean they could be counted on to acquit another tomorrow." He ran a finger over his moustache; I wanted to think he was cautioning himself against nodding. "But maybe there is something worse than lack of ambition. What about the ambitiousness fed to you like you feed a goose to fatten it up for the killing? You take it in because you have no choice."

"Who are we talking about, Robert?"

"Exactly," I had to laugh. "But leave me aside for a second. What I've learned about Salerno, there was never a goose more primed for the table. His family, the politics of the time. He was told what to aspire to before he ever knew what the possibilities were."

"And that makes him so unique?"

"I wouldn't go that far."

"Good. Because Saint-Cyr has graduated generations of policy makers, in and out of uniform. How many of them do you think *aspired* to go to Africa or Indochina when they entered the academy? They too were trained, force-fed in your language, in obligations, but that didn't make them any less effective in carrying them out. They were heroes, patriots."

"But Salerno didn't have that structure. He's always made it up as he's gone along."

He leaned over his folded arms expectantly. "Yes?"

"So have I, Commissioner. That's why I understand him. That's why I trust my intuition."

"So have you what? Made it up as you've gone along? Surely, you're joking."

Why couldn't he have taken it as one complete block of a confession instead of asking me to break it up in pieces? "I've never been quite as prepared as I give the impression of being. I've always had a nice quota of bluff in everything."

He still didn't move his arms. "And...?"

"And people who make up things as they go along, they often lose sight of the big picture. They're self-preoccupied. Their most conspicuous quality is narcissism. I'm not proud of it. I conceal it as much as possible. I hesitate to admit it to you right now. You cannot possibly think better of me for it." He didn't move a centimetre. "But every once in a great while, that limitation can be useful, perhaps even necessary, for concluding an inquiry. And when all is said and done, there remains a significant difference between me and Salerno. I work for the State. He not only works against it publicly, but of this I'm persuaded by now, in private lethal ways. And I'm the one adversary he fears most. He said as much with that note he sent me from the Hotel Avignon."

Blanc finally unfolded his arms and walked over to the window. I looked away before my imagination saw him opening the window and throwing Robert Frenaud's career down into the street.

"You think this strongly about Salerno you would make this admission you consider so potentially compromising?" he asked after a long moment.

"Yes."

What was I expecting? A reassurance I hadn't jeopardized my career? What I received was a low, building laugh and two dabs at his moustache. "Christ, Robert, I've underestimated you! Thank God your 'confession' isn't the kind we have to pass on the magistrature for indictment! We'd all be going out on fishing boats tomorrow morning! …All right, all right. You want to follow up on Salerno, follow up on him. But you're also going to do me a few favours when you go to Italy."

He was waiting for me to smile, to acknowledge a canniness I should have recognized as our mutual territory. But all I could think was that I had never felt so empty walking away from Father's Plesac's pew in the Sacré Coeur vestibule. Hadn't I been clear enough? What good was forgiveness for a sin that wasn't taken seriously?

Rachel was more merciful. Between the moment I told her of my new trip and my departure, she managed few words without an echo of impatience. There might have been more words but for a series of suddenly pressing engagements that coincided with my return home in the evening, a manicure at the most expensive salon in our district, a film with her best friend Yvette, a district association meeting to discuss the priorities of street lights and zebra crossings. Her evening returns were timed precisely for finding not only my meals for the children concluded, but all the dishes washed, dried, and back in the cabinet. To tell the truth, her hostility had a calming effect on me. Except for Janine's long, suspicious looks at me at the kitchen table one evening, I might have welcomed it altogether. Now nothing seemed to be in the way of finally confronting Salerno.

It seemed merely one more insignificant detail when, on my way out of the office the evening before my departure for Rome, Brunel handed me the positive identification of the woman found near Borgomanero. Not Patricia Mariani, but a Canadian national living in Philadelphia named Pamela Stubbs. I wondered who did my job in Borgomanero, and whether his official letter to Philadelphia would get somebody like Mario Salerno dropping by his office for a visit.

The rain thudded down with a demonic intensity at Fiumicino airport. As I stepped aboard the train for the ride to downtown Rome, I decided the weather was part of Blanc's price for the trip. It still seemed like a reasonable bargain. In exchange for having most of my arrival day and the afternoon of my fourth and final day free to look into Salerno, I really had to do only three things. Attend the Naples conference and listen to a lot of self-satisfied accounts of thwarting contraband gangs. Apologise without actually apologising to the Hamburg representative for a coordinated surveillance Blanc had personally compromised by blurting too much in a newspaper interview. And check in at the Viminale in Rome with one Sandro Codella, a Blanc equivalent in rank without whom I was not to lift a finger against Salerno. As a portly gentleman in the train seat behind finished shaking his raincoat over me, I couldn't imagine having negotiated better terms on my own. Not an hour of holiday time had been thrown into the pot.

The train deposited me near the unassuming hotel where Rachel and I had stayed on a vacation some years before. As one occupied taxi after another went sloshing past, I told myself that, whether I accomplished everything I could by nightfall or had to remain in the city for an early morning train to Naples, I would make a distant peace offering to Rachel by not requiring a hotel bed. I finally found a taxi and directed the driver to the Viminale Palace of the Interior Ministry. I had to admit a faint queasiness about dealing with Sandro Codella. Not only did he hold the equivalent of Blanc's rank, but he represented the home side for Salerno against outsiders with only their flimsiest of suspicions. And if, on top of everything else, the man also turned out to be a francophobe?

Commissario Sandro Codella didn't appear to be. Tall to the point of gangling, with a full black beard and sad, pouchy eyes, he welcomed me at the elevator on the third floor of the Viminale with a nonchalance I hardly associated with Blanc's professional equals. As he steered me through a maze of corridor desks and past a shouting match between two uniformed clerks, I found it hard to believe he was predisposed against anything but order and quiet. His office was about the size of Brunel's back in Rouen, and even a lot of that had been given over to banks of file cabinets and stacks of dossiers piled precariously against the walls. He saw my reaction as he waved me into a plastic bucket seat drawn up before the desk. "We do our best, and as you can see, our best is not nearly good enough."

"My office looks the same."

He smiled as he sat down. "Something tells me not. Aren't you damp in that jacket? Put it over the chair."

I did what he suggested, and instantly felt colder in my shirtsleeves. By way of compensation, he whipped out a cigarette and lighter from behind one of the paper piles on his desk. "Old Blanc says you smoke, but not my brand," he said, nudging a glass ashtray toward my side of the desk. "Perfect. You won't sit there resenting my weakness and I won't have to give you any of my cigarettes."

I didn't know whether I was more impressed by his casual tact or Blanc's knowledge of my brand.

"So Rouen is curious about Mario Salerno."

"More me than Rouen."

Codella mouthed his cigarette so that it jutted up from his beard; I made out pimples under the jaw hair. "The way Blanc explains it, you don't know exactly what you're looking for, but you'll know it when you see it."

"That's more optimistic than he sounded to me."

"He also added some disparaging remarks and numerous compliments about your abilities. I think they cancel each other out, leaving you as the sacrificial lamb for this Naples business tomorrow."

"Now you understand everything, Commissario."

He scrunched down further in his chair; only in repose did the older, mournful man who had received me at the elevator, look the thirty-five or thirty-six he probably was. "On to the juice of the matter then. Some American who killed himself in your city?"

I explained the situation as concisely as I could. He listened with an apprehensive curiosity until I got to Copenhagen, then he seemed to need the wall photo of the President of the Republic for a more meditated doubt. The Johnny Stuck story in Amsterdam dropped him into a still deeper hole, but I couldn't tell if his dolefulness was for human nature as a whole, Mario Salerno, or visiting Rouen policemen. When I finished, he gave me a long moment to be sure I was, flicked an ash in the general direction of the ashtray, and said: "I'm puzzled. This Salerno you describe from Copenhagen and Amsterdam, this man concealing something desperately, even murderously, just isn't the Salerno I recognise from here. You might as well tell me old Blanc is a playboy who dances away in nightclubs until dawn."

"We all have secret lives."

Codella matched my smile, but nothing else. "Let me tell you something about the intellectuals in this city, Frenaud," he said, waving in a uniformed officer with a tray of coffees. "First we have the impassioned kind ,the ones that were once very popular among the dissidents of the Left until the Communist Party disbanded and they had no more father to rebel against. These people can't give you traffic directions without hunching themselves into a ball and *arguing* with you about what streets to take to your destination. Then there are, what I call, the mummies. Most of them come from the university, the commentary pages of the press, the political think-tanks, the latest awards ceremony sponsored by the Vatican. They bray like goats, going on in some fiendish monotone that may or may not contain an idea, but that few people, apart from their sponsors and the wives of their sponsors, have the patience to listen to long enough to find out. Most of them also have some physical problem, like warts or bad breath. Right, Guarnieri?"

The officer smiled compliantly as he finished laying out the coffee and cups. "Whatever you say, Commissario."

"Good answer. Just make sure I don't hear myself being quoted the next time I go outside."

Guarnieri withdrew with a grin that said he couldn't wait to spread what he had heard from one end of the Viminale to the other. "Then there's a third type," Codella said, waiting an extra second for the office door to be closed. "They aren't impassioned or mummified. Think of them as polyester. They don't have organic resources, but they cover the situation. They pop up on television chairing round-tables and narrating documentaries. Open a book and you'll find they've written the preface. They introduce artists at openings and *engage* actors at press conferences. They make everything we hear interesting, but never threatening. They may speak about the homeless, the drug-addicted, the AIDS-afflicted, the starving masses in Africa, the roots of Moslem fundamentalism, or the hole in the ozone layer, but they make sure these topics are palatable to us. If they're thrown together with the impassioned, you can be sure they'll be adroit enough to penetrate the emotion and elicit whatever reason lurks beneath the sound and fury. When they find themselves trapped with the mummies, they'll display enough of their own passion to go on the attack and expose the depth of the decay next to them. They are always smart, frequently illuminating, and ultimately unobjectionable. They mean what they say for as long as they're saying it, then it's on to other things about which they feel equally earnest. Did I say polyester? No, think of them instead as mcs, masters of ceremonies, caterers. They serve up whatever seems important in a given moment, and with a zeal attesting to their competence, but they don't insist you pick up your fork to taste what they have laid out. That would imply some kind of responsibility on their part for the consequences of their actions. They don't want to hear about that. Once they've acquitted their function, they are indifferent to what ensues. *That* is Mario Salerno."

"You make that type sound placid. That's not the Salerno I know."

"Placidness. Smugness. You met him, what? Once?"

"If you don't count my manic reading of his collected works."

"Then you should know what I'm saying. Is there a controversial subject in thirty years he hasn't managed to sound like an expert about for a couple of hundred pages?"

"I'm talking more about his autobiographical things."

"There wasn't much of a readership for them here. A couple weren't even considered worthy of translation."

"But you seem familiar with them."

Codella reached over to pour the coffee. "Those files behind you against the wall? If some of our bright technocrats had their way, they would represent the last of the paper in this building. But there will always be paper, Frenaud, and as long as there is, we will always be reminded of how whimsical we've been about destroying our great forests. That first stack, nearest the door. Go ahead."

I knew what I was going to see before I got out of my chair and went over to the pile that came up to my knees. The top tab said SALERNO, MARIO, but it might as well have said ALL THE INFORMATION ROBERT FRENAUD WOULD HAVE DIED TO HAVE WEEKS AGO.

"After Blanc called, I thought I'd brush up on our subject before you started asking questions I couldn't answer. It's all on disc, of course, but I decided not to strain my eyes. Instead, I have three paper cuts to show for my industry on your behalf."

"May I look at them?"

"No, I had them brought up here because I was feeling lonely in this office. For Christ sake, man, there's a room next door! Bore yourself to tears with the activities of this intellectual caterer. Then we'll have lunch around the corner so you'll be able to say your trip wasn't completely wasted. Anything else?"

I reminded him about Leo Webber and Patricia Mariani. Seeing him note their names on a yellow pad and then pick up the phone to mention them to an assistant made me feel better. We were back to concrete police tasks.

The adjoining room, where Codella settled me with the Salerno files, was a windowless space with barely enough room for a bridge table and a couple of folding chairs. For all that, I felt a chill as soon as he closed the door on me. I didn't like my jacket still being draped over his chair next door, I didn't like his assumption I wouldn't need an ashtray, and I didn't like my sense of obligation in looking through ancient files that had nothing to do with why I had come to Rome. What the first half-dozen files amounted to were banal reports on Salerno's attendance at international conferences, copies of magazine articles, and a photograph of him sitting at a sidewalk table in the Piazza Navona with a middle-aged couple identified as SAHEEM HUSYANI AND HUSBAND, REPRESENTATIVES OF THE PALESTINIAN LIBERATION ORGANIZATION. I imagined Salerno and the Husyanis debating the relative merits of Italian *espresso* and the coffees to be had in the Middle East.

Then I imagined something funnier, what Codella had said about Blanc dancing away the wee hours in some night club. Picturing him gyrating his sacroiliac with some teenager with a ring in her belly button, made me feel giddy. Blanc would have needed a new body even to climb down the entrance steps of most Rouen nightclubs.

What did that have to do with Salerno sitting before my desk and discussing George Keller that first day? Only one thing: In striking one attitude with what he had been saying and another with his glassy look, he hadn't merely been disconnected, he had been *disembodied.*

I spent about an hour with the files, daring them to tell me something I wanted to know. With one exception, they failed. The exception was a dossier on Salerno's brother Giorgio, which tantalised me both for its bulk and for the premonition I'd had in Rouen that he would somehow prove illuminating. I forget now what they were, but I found several justifications for slipping that file into my bag for less rushed study.

Codella was in no hurry to ask my reactions to what I had read. First, he led me around the corner to a small *trattoria* that apparently specialised in vodka-laced rigatoni. Then there were his adventures with Blanc, back in the pre-Rouen days when Blanc had been in the political department of the Paris Sûreté. I needed little urging to listen to

Byzantine dramas of extradition requests for Italian neo-fascist terrorists, political pressures, bureaucratic snafus, and still more terrorist acts laid to the wanted criminals while French administrators like Blanc doggedly wound red tape around the most unimpeachable of warrants.

"The old fart was under orders to throw obstacles in our way, and he did a good job. As I remember, there were sixteen warrants sent to Paris, but only one of those bastards, the smallest of the small-timers and a cocaine addict besides, was ever returned to us. The other fifteen just happened to get to Spain or Morocco or Argentina before the French got around to knocking on their doors. Now I'm no romantic, Frenaud, but I think the old man thinks he owes me something from those unpleasant days, so I'm the first one he thinks of when he sends his best and brightest to Rome. Like the Chinese saying about being responsible for the man whose life you save. Blanc owes me, so I'm responsible for helping you."

"I wouldn't have taken you as someone with an Oriental view of things, Commissario."

He shrugged and took some wine. "What's the alternative? Blanc has come to associate me with stymied investigations and he'd like your inquiry into Salerno to be stymied?"

"That isn't possible!"

"That was a joke, Frenaud."

I felt like a damn fool. Codella had the grace to divert his attention to the arrival of our rigatoni and another half-carafe. I could only warn myself against confusing his sad countenance with a hapless mind.

"You don't like Salerno very much, do you?" he asked, as soon as the waiter had gone away.

"Like?"

He looked more tentative about his appreciation of the rigatoni than I was. "Like, dislike, a vital ingredient of some inquiries. Some years ago, we had a case involving smuggled diamonds from Israel. Everyone knew the merchandise was being moved through one of the old slaughterhouses on the Tiber, but we wasted forever trying to pinpoint which one. Even the Israelis began to lose interest for them. They bothered us about it every three hours instead of every hour. But I didn't lose interest. The reason I didn't was because of a third-rate thug named Beppe Farinelli. I hated Beppe Farinelli, Frenaud. I hated him when we were going to Blessed Heaven School, I hated him when he and his friends beat up my brother, and I hated him when I found out he'd got eleven-year-old Laura Petacca to jerk him off before she did it for me. So when I heard Beppe Farinelli was the owner of one of the slaughterhouses, I decided there was our target. The Israelis, everybody else, they were sceptical. A street-level extortionist? Cut-rate pimp? How did somebody running a few backroom roulette games get the clout for such a big diamond operation? I didn't know, I told them. But I knew he was involved."

"And was he?"

"Of course not," he shrugged into his plate. "We turned him and his slaughterhouse upside down and inside out, but we found nothing. He's still over in Testaccio today running his whores and crap games."

I was supposed to say something, so I did. "The dangers of tainting legal recourse with personal spite."

"No, the dangers of legal recourse *not catching up to* personal spite. You not only have to trap the man, you have to concoct the reason making him vulnerable to the trap. I wasn't patient enough to do that."

My anger rose so fast my arm muscles began to twitch. "Whatever Blanc told you about my feelings about Salerno, Commissario...

"Give me your glass and stop reminding yourself of my rank. All men are equal before their Maker and their silverware. That's why we're having this talk here and not back in my office."

"I can assure you…"

He clunked the carafe back down on the table. "Please don't," he said with a new sharpness. "Leave the assuring to me. We're in Rome now, not Rouen. And because you strike me as a serious man, I'll help you. But I too have records to keep. For example, Salerno may be one of those polyester intellectuals I mentioned, but he still titillates many people, still boasts acquaintances of some influence. Worse for me, most of them own phones, computers and fax machines. You follow me?"

"Of course."

"I hope so because some things don't change. Once upon a time, the Communists held grand rallies at San Giovanni. More recently, we have Britney Spears giving concerts there. Either way they've needed street sweepers afterward, and I'm not ready for the job. Follow that, too?"

I did.

And decided he was right about the rigatoni. It was just the slightest bit overcooked.

My reward came when we returned to the Viminale. Even as I was dreading another couple of hours going through the motions with the Salerno files in the claustrophobic box next to Codella's office, he scanned a piece of paper left on his desk and handed it to me. "Your Leo Webber seems to be alive and well," he said. "I'll have Guarnieri accompany you, with instructions to stay in the background. If you need him, just signal."

The sheet of paper said Webber had been tracked down to a *pensione* in the Piazza Vittorio where a woman named Antonacci had directed a police team to the Stazione Termine. Of course, it was good news that no harm had come to Webber. But it would have been better news if that fact hadn't prompted Codella to look at me even more sceptically.

Leo Webber was an American track-and-field fantasy: tall, slender, blue eyes, the kind of long blond hair that would have flown up as he crossed a finish line. How else should he have been togged out than in white jeans, a T-shirt with the blue and white of some Los Angeles sports team, white sweat socks, and white canvas shoes?

What wasn't so natural was that a 25-year-old American should be hustling customers at the central Rome train station.

"It's simple," he shrugged, tinkering with his cappuccino spoon at the table we had taken at the station café. "When there's a train from Milan or points north, I just wander over to the gate there and plant myself. Don't solicit, don't open my mouth. I just stand there so all the tourists getting off can see me. And if one of them decides I look like a trustworthy American, he'll ask me if I can direct him to a good hotel or *pensione*."

"And you do."

He lifted a heavy finger toward the kiosk at the other end of the gallery. "Fulvio Antonacci's," he said, indicating a diminutive crow of a man in a heated argument with two capped hotel touts. "Cheapest rooms in Rome."

"An original way to see the city."

He returned his eyes to the foam on his spoon. "My own idiocy. Soon as I arrived, I got my bags stolen. I had nothing left but the clothes on my back. Then I ran into Fulvio, and he offered me food and a bed if I came down here with him to attract some American customers."

"Can't you borrow some money so you won't be stuck here?"

"Did I say I was stuck?" Even without reminding himself who I was, it came out too heavily. "Okay, it's a question I ask myself every day. I tell myself I'm resting up to go back to the States to star in some brilliant new play. I know, you wouldn't have taken me for an actor. Not too many producers have, either."

I wasn't in the mood for what sounded like weeks of dammed up conversation. "So let's go back to George Keller."

"I told you, I don't know the man."

"And that's all you thought when you received my letter? You didn't know him, so into the garbage with the letter?"

His eyes wandered impatiently toward where Guarnieri was pretending interest in a train schedule, then left and right again. "Look, I picked it up at the Post Office, I went back to Fulvio's, I ran down everybody I could think of. Nobody from my family or school. No-one I met in New York. Then I thought back to one of my actor-lives in San Francisco, but the best I came up with there was an old man who used to come to our shows because he said I reminded him of his dead son. Keller wasn't a 70-year-old tailor, was he?"

"No."

There you are, then. Just like I told Salerno."

"And he believed you?"

"Why not? It's the truth."

"I'm sure it is. But still I find it odd that, stranded as you are here, you could act so casual about receiving a letter like that."

He didn't begrudge me the thought. "Okay. Maybe it did get to me some. But not because of this Keller. I thought about that old tailor in California and that got me thinking about all the bad plays I was in out there featuring Leo Webber in alphabetical order. Once I started thinking about those days, I thought about all the mornings I'd had to boil myself a potato for breakfast, all those rainy nights under the

135

Stockton Street tunnel, all the Born-Agains who slept with me to do Christ's work, and all my other Aladdin adventures out there. I suppose Keller came in second best."

"So second you couldn't find the curiosity to answer the letter."

"I had nothing to say to you!"

"You could've told me I'd made a mistake."

"But maybe you didn't! Maybe Keller was a friend of a friend of a friend who never mentioned him to me. He *did* have my address, didn't he? There was just nothing I could've said to you."

I could hear Salerno asking the same question I did: "So it wasn't worth following up on the off-chance you had, say, an inheritance waiting for you in Rouen?"

He tried to look amused; and was definitely hiding something. "Make me laugh some more."

"I see. So what I'm supposed to believe is that this actor with lots of time on his hands gets this strange letter, thinks about it for a few minutes, then decides it's not half as fascinating as drowning in your self-pity with that character over there."

If he was ever going to bolt, that was the moment. But Leo Webber merely thought about how offended he should have been, then drained his cappuccino. "Okay," he shrugged. "I thought, 'Special Agent Leo Webber plugs into Central Records and gets all the computer screens lighting up on George Keller.' That better?"

"Like a film."

"Right. The one where I mosey up to Rouen, find out Keller was really my father, and was murdered before he could say who killed the Kennedys, Martin Luther King, and Abe Lincoln. I end up unmasking the killer, but then I get shot for my trouble, too."

His defiantly vulnerable stare made me think of Andre Lafont; the Parisian student had also resented his imagination and wanted others to resent him for it as well. "That what you told Salerno?"

His sudden whoop made the couple at the next table jump and brought an alarmed lurch from Guarnieri. "Christ, he was worse than you! We sat here at the same table. Practically the same questions."

"Better answers, I hope."

"Look, captain, inspector…"

"Inspector is fine."

He hunched closer to the table; he was supposed to be more sincere. "I get your letter, okay? Then I get Salerno here and now it's you. Most action I've had in months. But this doesn't have my name on it any more than creating a future around Fulvio Antonacci's bed-and-breakfast does. I told Salerno that and I'm telling you. Maybe one day, thirty years from now, an old friend from New York will drop Keller's name and I'll have the mystery of your letter cleared up. If you think it's worth waiting that long, give me your address and I'll drop you a line then."

What Salerno would have reminded himself, I was sure, was that Webber was an actor. "What did Salerno say when you told him that?"

He had expected more from his great show of earnestness. "Like I didn't appreciate the fact we'd both won some lottery… No. More like we'd won a lottery by getting your letter, but forget about the prize. Why couldn't I be as interested as he was in working out the scientific laws that'd made our tickets topple over millions of others to get picked. Spooky."

"Excuse me?"

"Spooky. Eerie. Weird."

A red light went on next to the train due from Amsterdam. Worse, the crow named Antonacci had broken off his argument with the hotel touts and was looking at his watch. "Let's go for a walk, Leo," I said grabbing the bill from the table. "We won't be long. You should miss only your Amsterdam train. If your friend Fulvio has a problem with that, there's an officer standing over there at the arrivals board who can explain things to him."

I looked up only when the dismay was already receding from his face. "But there's nothing else I can tell you!"

"Why don't we decide that as we go along?"

I left too much money with the waiter, but rationalised I hadn't paid for lunch and would save again by not spending on a Rome hotel for the night. Where was I taking the American? I had no idea, other than to get him away from the interruption sure to come from his *pensione*-keeper. I also wanted to get away from the spectres his every moment in the station seemed to summon forth. The sheer absurdity of the penniless American actor buttonholing train passengers for his survival made me think of hordes of American misfits descending on the continent and wreaking havoc from the English Channel to the Urals. Only the most despondent of them seemed to jump off hotel ledges in Rouen.

The afternoon air was humid, surly in its anticipation of another downpour. I didn't want to meander, but I didn't want Webber seeing my agitation, either. "How did you and Salerno part company?"

"He invited me to dinner."

"Did you go?"

"You kidding? Fulvio's wife is a great cook, but you can get tired even of Julia Child twice a day seven days a week."

"Where did you go?"

Away from the station, obviously. Somewhere where, if Salerno had heard the wrong answer, it would have been easier to deal with Webber. Obviously, though, he hadn't heard a wrong answer. "He asked you about Patricia Mariani?"

Webber pulled back at the corner, but not because the traffic light told him to wait. "That her name? He kept circling around some woman he seemed to think Keller and I both should have known. But every time I asked what her name was, he said it wasn't important. Who is she?"

The light changed, and he had to follow me across old tram tracks further away from the station. There it was, of course: the first evidence from Salerno's mouth that Mariani was the key to everything. "It isn't important."

He thought I was being funny again. "Got you."

"So you haven't seen Salerno since this dinner, that it?"

Broodier thoughts. "He promised to hook me up with some friend of his who does English voiceovers, but that was last week and I haven't heard from him. I think I'm going to have to settle for getting a dinner out of it."

And for keeping his life. But why tell him that when he was still withholding something from me? "Let's backtrack a second, Leo. You told him about your little movie fantasy. Then he impressed you with this glee about winning a lottery ticket. But that's not where your conversation about George Keller stopped. You told him something else you haven't told me yet... Please. Keep walking. And no more evasions."

There was another silence for the length of three storefronts. Then the announcement: "There's another Leo Webber." He looked so soulful about what he considered an admission I wanted to laugh. "It's the flaw in their post office system! You go up to the mail counter, you flash your passport, then you take away anything addressed to the passport name. No one worries about the chance there're two William Smiths, or two Leo Webbers ,looking for mail in the same city at the same time!"

"Because it *is* unlikely."

"Sure. And that's what the post office woman said to me. 'Which Leo Webber was I?' 'Could I prove I was this Leo Webber and not that one?'"

"You took the letter, Leo."

"Sure. I liked getting it. I liked making that movie in my mind. To hell with that other Leo Webber and his right to mourn one of his suicidal pals. This was *my* adventure we were talking about! What else mattered?"

I didn't want to believe that was his dark secret, nor accept that Salerno had apparently swallowed it so gullibly.

"I'm telling you, Frenaud," he said, entertained by my expression. "There's another Leo Webber and he's probably a long way from Rome by now. He sure hasn't answered my note."

"What note?"

"I left him a note with your letter at the post office," he shrugged. "Every day I go down there I have to refuse to take it. It's still sitting there in one of their pigeonholes."

"You told Salerno this?"

He laughed more easily. "Only after our dinner. I figured if I said anything at the train station, he might not be so hot to invite me. But do you hear me, Frenaud? Dead or alive, George Keller is a total stranger to me. *I invented my part in all this!*"

People were hurrying up and down the sodden asphalt past us. They looked stuck with the umbrellas they had needed earlier. Across the street, a chunky brunette, in a lime dress under a white smock, was unlocking the window guard of a toy store for a small boy and his grandfather. As soon as she removed the screen, the boy let go of his grandfather's hand and ran to the window for a closer look at what had tickled his fancy. I couldn't grasp why, if the intention had been to give the boy a closer look at some toy, the salesgirl hadn't simply taken it from the window and handed it to him.

"There's nothing else I can tell you!"

How many times had I heard that, not just from him, but from Jill Faber, Andre Lafont, and others? But none of them had wound up in Keller's red address book as he had. "So Keller isn't connected to someone you knew in America. What about over here?"

"Who? Fulvio at the *pensione*?"

There was every reason to let the smug question pass. But the best reason not to, was the narrow, raised entrance to a dry goods store next to us. Not counting a few pulls and shoves when I had been in uniform, I had never assaulted a suspect, and had made a point of instructing Josselin, Brunel, and my other assistants never to go beyond the occasional shouldering to speed up an interrogation. But as I nudged Webber into the tiled entrance of the draper's, seeing two clerks busy inside with customers, I felt just exasperated enough, just damp enough in my jacket, and just distended enough from my lunch wine to smash his head against the display window until he told me what I wanted to know. As soon as he realised he was so backed into the furthest corner of the entrance that passers-by couldn't see us unless they stopped and craned their necks, panic glinted in his eyes. "I've got no reason not to tell you!"

"I asked you about the people you've met here."

"Tourists, for Christ sake!"

"Who were they?"

He gave up trying to look over my shoulder to the street. "Two girls from Wisconsin, okay? Barbara and Page. No, they weren't this Mariani. They weren't remotely Italian. A basketball player who's going to study medicine in Bologna. An ornithologist guy, talked all the time about egrets."

"What are egrets?"

"Birds. Keller have birder friends?"

His bafflement overwhelmed my resolve; I didn't even feel like whacking him gratuitously. "They were all Americans?"

"Mostly. There was a German pair, a composer and his wife. All that stuff where you crunch up potato chip bags and go, 'Hey, great music!' And one of the first ones I picked up was French. He didn't know what egrets were either, but he spent four days making it clear he was doing me a big favour by letting him learn English words like that."

One of the clerks was approaching the door to see what the commotion was about. "French, you say?"

"Guy with a real attitude. He barely had enough to cover one of Fulvio's rooms, but that didn't stop him from patronising me, Fulvio, Fulvio's wife, and everybody else at the *pensione*. He also thought I was on twenty-four-hour call as his private guide around the city. All Frenchmen like that or you specialise in it at Paris art schools?"

I didn't dare move even as the store clerk gaped out at us and put his hand on the inside doorknob. I had spent so much time looking for connections between George Keller and the names in his address book that I hadn't prepared myself for actually discovering one. "The Frenchman," I heard myself, "was his name Lafont, Andre Lafont?"

Webber was too stunned to warn the clerk that the badge I flashed had no authority in Italy. "Yes," he managed to say. "Andre Lafont."

I laughed at the clerk's decision not to look at my badge too closely and to withdraw from the door, who cared who got beat up on his doorstep. At Leo Webber's bewilderment. At all the time I had spent listening to the wrong parts of Andre Lafont's interrogation, completely ignoring the little snob's allusion to having recently visited Rome. But also at something else. It seemed never to have occurred to Leo Webber, American actor playing the part of a Rome hustler, that he hadn't invented a connection to George Keller and Mario Salerno, that the only thing he had invented with the creation of a second Leo Webber was his own imagination.

Codella was impressed, and so was Josselin. The commissario stared at me pensively from behind his desk while I instructed Josselin to confirm Webber's story with Lafont. They had no more doubts than I did that Lafont had given Webber's address to George Keller on the assumption the painter would have needed a place to stay in Rome, but I wanted every last *t* crossed.

"Of course you still have two big question marks," Codella said as soon as I hung up.

"Why kill himself if he had a specific destination."

He lit a cigarette and extinguished his match with a wide, lazy wave through the air. "That's one, yes."

I had no answer to that, at least outside the scenario suggested by Lafont. George Keller had been suddenly overwhelmed by some sense of detachment and had blithely walked over to the window of the Flamant.

"Assuming you've ruled out foul play, I don't think you're ever going to get an answer to that one."

"No, no foul play. Maybe he killed himself on the spur of the moment, maybe he didn't. Maybe he was sincerely thinking about coming to Italy, maybe he was just being polite when Lafont gave him Webber's name. I don't think that part of it matters anymore except as a link to Mariani."

Codella agreed and didn't agree; that part of it wasn't within his responsibility. But the second question mark still was. "You have her in Milan and you have Salerno down here at this conference about displaced peoples. You still haven't connected those dots for me, Frenaud."

"And your people still haven't found her."

Had I meant it as criticism? Of course I had. But it still came out too thickly, and he abruptly lost his leisurely interest in his cigarette. "I think you better watch your trains," he said, pushing himself into his computer. "If we discover your missing Mariani, we know where to find you in Naples. *Buon viaggio*, Frenaud."

I spent the first morning session of the Naples conference wishing all the seas and rivers of Europe would dry up. There was so much infinitesimal data about contraband patterns, all of it dispatched through a defective microphone at the front of a sweltering amphitheatre, that, Salerno or not, I found it easy to resent Arnaud's conscientious reasons for getting out of the assignment. Finally, though, came an announcement of a fifteen-minute break before a report on the police role in harbour ecology. I wasted little of it scrambling down from my back row seat, smiling emptily at a Finnish delegate I almost knocked over as she was rising from her aisle place, and hurrying out to the telephone at the reception desk. I might have run even faster if I had known what was awaiting me.

"Nothing yet on Mariani," Codella began droopily. "Maybe not all roads lead to Rome, after all. What do you think?"

What I had been thinking since sitting in my compartment on the train from Rome to Naples. "The usual hotel checks may be a waste of time."

He laughed, and not altogether pleasantly. "Salerno's apartment? We've already talked to the *portiere* there. Nobody. Nothing."

I had coddled that idea too long overnight to hear it rejected so nonchalantly. But then everything else became unimportant. "Your office called this morning before I got in," Codella said. "You've received a letter they thought was urgent enough to fax on to you here. I'm looking at it right now and I think they have a point."

I had no doubt of the letter writer. "Salerno?"

"I'll fax it down to you," he said, as though edgy about saying yes or no. "What's your number there?"

I pulled out the conference schedule I had stuffed into my pocket. A fax number was tucked away at the bottom of an endless list of organisation credits. I lingered near the reception desk, and the fax machine, while the other delegates trooped back into the amphitheatre. By the time the letter came, an usher was closing the door of the conference room. I brought the letter over to a bench before the floor's only window and sat down with it. Even through smeared fax toner the typing looked neat and precise.

Dear Frenaud,

I'm afraid I haven't been completely frank about my relationship to George Keller. I can only claim as an excuse some lingering doubts of my own about it while I was in Rouen. But however that might be, I feel it is my obligation to your investigation and to you personally to share with you what I have come to confirm as the reason for my name appearing in Keller's address book.

What I have now ascertained to my satisfaction is this: Keller was an acquaintance of a woman I have known most of my life. It was she who felt free to give him my Rome address, presumably so I could play a pliant host as he regaled me with his experiences as one of her extremely temporary lovers. In this, Keller would have been merely the latest in a steady wave of drifters my friend has seen fit to unfurl on me for all the Roman amenities I can supply.

Why the trip to Rouen? Simply because I'd had enough. For years, I have been imploring my friend not to hand out my Rome address as though she were passing out flyers on a street corner, but without success. Not to put too fine a point on it, your letter caused me to snap. If Keller had my home address, how many people had he in turn given it to? It had become intolerable to open my door and come face to face with some stranger who acted beyond irritated when just mentioning my friend's name didn't earn him a welcoming hug and my offer to clear my stuff out of my bedroom for him. For once, I thought, I would snuff out that migration toward Casa Salerno at its disembarkation point.

Granted Rouen doesn't answer exactly to that description. But I trust you grasp my meaning. When you grow weary of fighting unwanted battles on your doorstep, the temptation in a moment of fragility is to run across the street pre-emptively and display all your vulnerabilities there. As you can attest, it was certainly my temptation. At the moment, I have far too much on my plate without having to worry about all the George Kellers of the world ringing my bell at the most unexpected moments. There is nothing at all flattering about being out of control, Frenaud, but there it is.

I hope this clears up one of the details that has prevented you from consigning the Keller file to your cellar archives. Beyond that, I would like to believe the time has come for all of us to allow the wretched Keller to rest in peace. Surely, that was all he wanted, or felt capable of, when he stepped out on the ledge of the Hotel Flamant. Let us give the dead their due.

Indebted for your understanding,
Mario Salerno

I read the entire letter a second time, then the signature three or four times. He was still *indebted* to me, I could hear Jens Madsen yelling in my ear. And that was only the beginning.

I wanted to sense the lies before actually singling them out, so I first disposed of what was true. Keller *had* obtained Salerno's address through Mariani. He obviously *had* gone to Rouen in some sort of panic. He *didn't* want anybody else showing up on his doorstep through the good offices of Keller or Mariani. But after that?

The reference to being too busy to contemplate unannounced visitors? Not exactly a hundred per cent lie, more like an ordinary profession of self-importance, since he had always been involved in things like conferences on displaced peoples. But at the very least a contradiction before the fact that, arduous schedule or not, he had found the time to go not only to Rouen, but to Copenhagen and Amsterdam, as well.

Inconclusive. Dissembling wasn't quite an explicit lie.

I lay the letter on the bench for more distance. And immediately, the sun coming through the high window showed me where I should have been looking. How had he learned from Mariani that she had passed on his address to Keller? When had he spoken with her? Where had he spoken with her? Before or after he had received my letter and travelled to Rouen? To believe him, it had been after, when, according to Josselin's information from New York, Mariani should have been in Europe. Did I dare believe him?

Then the sun reminded me of the second lie. The letter itself! And, feeling something knot in my stomach, not just Mario Salerno's. Why feel compelled to get in touch with me unless cautioned to do so? I thought of Codella, Guarnieri, other faces in the corridors and elevators of the Viminale. And even that was a waste of grey matter. Anybody at all in the building who had heard about the reasons for my visit, a switchboard operator, could have set into motion the network of telephones, e-mails, and faxes for warning Salerno and advising him how to proceed.

Their advice? Evidently, don't wait for Frenaud to walk up to your door. Take pre-emptive action with him, too.

They were afraid. Of what?

I pocketed the letter before I had to follow that line of thought too far. Mariani to Keller to Salerno, that was what I had to focus on, what I wished Emile Josselin was around to help me focus on. What exactly did I have in my pocket? Anxiety? Not a crime. A sense of guilt? Not a crime. The letter itself, with all its equivocations and presumed indebtedness to me? Definitely a crime. But needing to be proven.

I couldn't think of a good alternative to slipping back inside the amphitheatre. I certainly didn't want to wander around Naples chewing the letter flavourless. I wanted it to settle, persuade me after an hour or two that I had indeed been handed vital evidence. I found a seat next to the raven-haired Finn I had almost knocked over in my haste to get out of the auditorium at the break. She pretended not to recognise me. She had a cherry scent and was wearing a nondescript white blouse, navy skirt, and black loafers. I imagined her wearing a white bra and sensible white panties. She looked bored with the tall, horse-faced Swede who was lecturing on the allies and enemies to be distinguished in the struggle for cleaner ports. I was certainly bored having to listen to one speaker after another through a microphone that was half-echo and half-whistle.

"Excuse me!"

The Swede peered up from his manuscript mid-sentence, didn't seem to know if he was annoyed or amused. "We really can't hear you," I told him, surprised at how truly impatient I had become. "Can't you repair that microphone or get another one?"

He was only too happy to twist his awkward body around to the organisers sitting at the table next to the lectern. It took a bald-headed wrestler of a man a very long moment to acknowledge he was the one with the ultimate responsibility for technical matters. Only as he stood and took me in dubiously did heads start turning in my direction. "Is the delegate from Rouen having trouble understanding?"

Condescension has always seemed more tolerable when I was on the bestowing end. "We're talking about simple hearing! With all the work that has gone into preparing this conference, all the money spent by our cities to send representatives, is it really asking too much that we have a microphone that works properly?"

I saw some nods out of the corner of my eye, mainly from those without headphones, but not enough to make me feel like Robespierre at the National Convention. What was more reassuring was the energetic agreement of the Finn. As though she had been waiting all along to voice a protest, she jumped to her feet and waved her arm dramatically around the amphitheatre. "You want to share your views on port city problems, but you do not permit us even to hear them!" she cried in an angrily precise English. "Who has organized this conference, the people responsible for the problems?"

There was scattered laughter around the room. The wrestler looked befuddled, and the Swede was content to leave him looking like that. Somewhere in Helsinki, I thought, there was a husband who would hear about his wife's affair with me in Naples, then start tearing around the continent to look up every conference delegate to make sure nobody could spread word of his humiliation.

"You are absolutely right!" she turned to me, her face red with indignation.

There wasn't a trace of flirtation in the compliment. She really *was* just furious about the goddam microphone!

Rachel made only one crack about my *dolce vita*. Roger sounded mainly peeved to be summoned to the phone from his bedroom. Janine protested my 'another day or two', but seemed mollified when I promised her a day together without her mother or brother. Only after hanging up did I remember the call from Roger to my office while I had been in Denmark. I had never got to the bottom of that crisis, if indeed it had been one.

Still, leaving Naples before the final conference session and checking into a modest hotel behind the Pantheon had seemed right. Calling Blanc and Rachel to warn them of that extra day or two in Rome had seemed right. Even trusting that Codella hadn't been the cause of Salerno's letter had seemed right. Especially with his pointed suggestion that, if I wanted to sample Rome's sidewalk bar life, I should try the café directly across from Tre Scalini in the Piazza Navona. "If you'd paid more attention to those files," he had said, pointing to the reassembled stacks on the floor in his office, "you'd have noticed Salerno's crusades have changed over the years, but not his patronage of certain bars."

Was I ready to re-encounter Salerno with what I had? That had been the gist of Codella's challenge. How else could I have responded than to meander over to the Piazza Navona that evening and take a conspicuous seat before the arcaded building housing the bar? It took me an iced coffee to feel part of the practiced chaos around me rather than its target, then half of another to accept that everyone walking past wasn't some kind of advance scout for Salerno. I began to study the tourists who strolled up to the café, looked hesitant about committing themselves to a table, then wandered off again. I watched two Somalis promoting their chainware on the pedestrian island around the centre fountain. I thought about Rachel and her insinuations about how hard it had been for her family in Algeria, and was annoyed it had taken Salerno's visit to Rouen for her to allude to a dark story she had never told me in detail (and that maybe I hadn't really wanted to know). I thought of Ari Kekkonen in Naples, and wished I had suggested getting a drink. It had been a long time since I had been to bed with a woman who, even for a day, was under the impression I was 'absolutely right' about something.

Then I saw Salerno.

Clearly, his letter was supposed to have erased me from his life forever. He needed all his willed composure to squeeze out something like a smile and to stop the woman next to him with a hand to her elbow. As I stood to shake hands, I thought I was giving away as much as he was. I decided I wasn't when he was the one to propose sitting at my table. Whatever I was actually showing, it took me a minute or two to get over my disorientation. For weeks, I had been preoccupied with Mario Salerno, but the Salerno of books, scribbled notes, and the testimonies of people who had known next to nothing about him. The heavyset man pulling up the legs of his tan slacks as he tried to get comfortable in the tight café chair was a much older, more aggressive Salerno, the one who ages ago had marched into my office to tell me how to do my job. This was again the closer-to-seventy-than-to-sixty, Perry Mason actor from television, the one with the liquid eyes, the one who treated the words out of his mouth as distant concessions to society that the mind behind them would never contemplate making.

Not that there hadn't been changes. Maybe it was the taut-skinned woman's presence, but he seemed whiter around the temples, pouchier in the face. There was a sluggishness to his movements I didn't recall from my office. How else to say it but that he simply looked his age?

"And what was this conference all about?"

I told him; or better, I told Carla Vianello because it seemed like the smoothest way of keeping my eyes off him. Carla Vianello was a striking woman in her forties, in a white shirt and black Capri pants, just short of a glossy magazine's idea of middle-aged slimness and vivacity, and for that lack more interesting than any periodical could manufacture. She had a rasp I could imagine sounding pugnacious, but also an easy smile that congratulated people for being intelligent enough to humour her. I was slinking toward finding out how close they were as friends when Salerno simply told me.

"Married?" I stammered.

He was amused. "The inspector seems to think you shouldn't tie yourself down to an old man, Carla."

The arrival of the waiter relieved her from having to comment. She ordered two gin and tonics with nothing more than a consenting nod from Salerno. I didn't need to order anything else. It had been given to me without having to ask: the reason, George Keller hadn't been just one more drifter sent to Rome by Patricia Mariani. There was no way cousin

Patti and her incidental friends were going to upset Mario Salerno's marriage!

"Actually, Frenaud, if you're going to be here tomorrow, you're welcome to join the celebration."

I was speechless. I thought of Madeline Bendel, of the desperate bravado she had once hurled across a courtroom at me after my testimony against her, crying out I would be the guest of honour at her acquittal party. There would be no wedding for Salerno, I told myself, as there had been no acquittal party for Madeline Bendel.

"Maybe the inspector has other commitments, Mario. Would you have a cigarette, Inspector? I seem to be out."

"Not your brand," Salerno said before I had even reached into my pocket. "The *tabaccaio* is open. I'll be right back."

One clumsiness followed another. As Salerno popped out of his seat, I was on the brink of telling him not to move, realised I had no authority or even evidence for such a command, then practically barked she take my brand anyway. Both of them looked at me oddly. Then he went off toward the tobacco shop some doors up the square anyway, and she poised her fingers over my package anyway, and I shook a cigarette loose for her anyway. "I haven't tried these in a long time. Forgive Mario. He's always doing that."

"Excuse me?"

"Your brand," she said, taking my light. "You've met what, once or twice? He has a memory for the smallest things."

Salerno had reached the tobacco shop and was permitting a couple to precede him through the door. If they were served first, I had about three minutes. "He could have noticed my butts here in the ashtray."

She smiled. She was uncomfortable with me, but I couldn't believe it was because she knew something specific about Patricia Mariani. "Of course. Maybe I'm trying too hard to impress you with my husband-to-be."

I hoped Rachel would forgive me. "He's fortunate. One day I hope to meet a woman who would like to impress people with me. Or is that what all marriages are supposed to be?"

She was finally relaxed enough to unharness her shoulder bag and stick it on her lap. "It's supposed to start with love, isn't it?"

"So they say."

Too heavy. "Well, *they* are right for once."

"I see."

"You concede that like it's a disturbing notion."

"Maybe just envy."

She was sceptical, but didn't know about what. I counted off too many seconds while the waiter made a show of setting out their drinks and sticking a bill under Salerno's glass. On the other hand, nobody had emerged yet from the tobacco shop. "Tell me his secret," I said, as soon as the waiter had left.

She smiled to the curl of her smoke. "I could say good taste on his part. But I think we just found each other after a long time of not seeing each other or only thinking of one another as oases on separate trails."

"So I better pay more attention to my secretary." Everything that came out was oafish.

"I'm not talking about settling for somebody... Yes, that's what you meant. Some of our friends think that way, too."

"You don't bother to correct them?"

"I'm marrying Mario, not them." She glanced down at the tobacco shop; the couple Salerno had let enter ahead of him came out. "You have me gabbing very quickly, Inspector. Is this a Rouen police technique?"

"Not one I've been conscious of."

It wasn't half as clumsy as what else I had been saying, but there was a new edge in her look at me. "Know what I believe in more than any other single thing, Inspector

Frenaud? I believe in stories. I believe in the stories your father read to you when you went to bed. All those fantasies about witches and dragons and the handsome princes and beautiful princesses. I believe in those stories because I never would have gone to sleep without them. I believe in them because that's what you wake up from the next morning as an adult who wants to share her life with someone who also believed in those stories and who also knows he wouldn't have been able to go to sleep without them and who also wants to get on with things. No, Mario and I aren't settling for one another. We're both just waking up in the same bed at the same time and we both like what it feels like."

Salerno emerged from the store with several packs of cigarettes in his meaty hands. Even if he had still been inside, I wouldn't have been able to answer the woman. She had embarrassed me twice over, by telling me more than I'd had a right to hear and by being totally indifferent to my deceit. I hoped I wouldn't see her again after Patricia Mariani's body was found.

"In case you run out," Salerno said, depositing two packs in front of me. "No, no, you're the guest here. So, have you decided? Will you join us at the Campidoglio at three o'clock tomorrow?"

"You're pushing, Mario," she said, sweeping her packs into her bag.

"Nonsense," he said, taking his gin and tonic. "If he's here tomorrow, there's no reason he can't come. Frenaud?"

Even thinking again about Madeline Bendel didn't help. "I'll be in Rome tomorrow, yes."

Salerno tried to look satisfied as he sipped his drink. Carla Vianello thought about reminding him I hadn't said yes or no, then changed her mind in favour of getting rid of my cigarette for one of her own.

I couldn't sleep that night. I blamed everything: the stifling hotel room, the incessant gurgling of water through the pipes outside my alley window, the iced coffees from the Navona bar. All beside the point, of course. The only reason I couldn't sleep was that *everything was over*. I was through with Salerno's books, with his cryptic letters, with all the people with whom he had crossed paths. He had thrown Leo Webber a vague promise about voiceover work? Surely, that had been connected to Carla Vianello's position at the state television network. No detail, trivial or significant, was beyond me for recommending his arrest to Codella.

If only I knew where Patricia Mariani's body was.

As I stared off at the flaking hotel room wall, I thought of a toy in my father's department store. It had been called One-Two-Three, and had been little more than a large wooden box studded with dozens of coloured buttons on all sides. The idea had been to press the right combination of three and only three buttons so that the box would fly open and the Tricolour spring out. I had thought it an idiotic toy, absolutely useless as soon as the right combination (the colours of the national flag) was pressed the first time. Nevertheless, whenever my mother had taken me to the store to pick up my father in the evening, I had invariably gravitated toward the aisle with One-Two-Three in order to sneak in a few pokes at the box. Then one evening, my father had caught me at it, not knowing that I had long since resolved the key. "Again," he had said, sounding mainly like a doctor asking to repeat a cough for evaluation. "Again, Robert."

To make him feel better, I had jabbed at the wrong buttons for a minute or so. "You're not thinking," he had said, his gaze fixed more on the box than on me. "You should be intelligent enough to eliminate all but three of those buttons right away." When I had finally ended the charade to press the Tricolour buttons, he had nodded approvingly. "Remember always to take an extra minute to understand the problem," he had said. "Problems usually contain their own solutions."

Lying in my muggy hotel room, I could still feel a little tremor at how I had deceived my father that night. But I was also assailed by a doubt that I had taken that extra minute. Something besides the whereabouts of Patricia Mariani's body still seemed to be eluding me. Then I remembered Giorgio Salerno and I popped up from the bed the way the Tricolour had once jumped out of the One-Two-Three box.

I pushed the room's single chair as close to the window as I could for some air, grabbed my cigarettes and the Giorgio Salerno dossier I had borrowed from Codella, and flopped down. On paper, the brother who had always been such a *bête noire* for Salerno sounded like just another ex-partisan who had aged gracelessly through decades of potentially troubling, but ultimately innocuous, political events. On public occasions, at rallies and demonstrations, in petition signings and letters to the editor and scolding notes to Communist Party functionaries, he had been redder than the Communists and even many of the splinter groups that had broken off to their left; in short, without an effective place on the political spectrum, so completely laid over himself as to have become a black hole. In private, in the stability of his real estate business, in his tangential role in the 1974 trafficking of some Etruscan statuary, in an ancient affair with a woman who years later had risen to the presidency of the Italian House of Deputies, he had bobbed up and down in a sea of banality. Giorgio Salerno had never been a threat to anybody, but a forest of trees had been required for noting that fact. Typical, absurdly so, was an entry from the Political Section of the Interior Ministry, dated April 1991:

G.V. Salerno was overheard the afternoon of April 18 at the Bar Diamante, Via Castilla 89, telling several patrons he was going to create his own Communist Party

in Italy. He said his party would ban all goods from the United States, including films and television programmes. He said he would ban all Russian products too, though he doubted anyone would notice their absence. The bar patrons laughed, but G.V. Salerno insisted he was serious. One patron, a market vendor known locally as Er Cervellone, volunteered to be G.V. Salerno's first recruit. G.V. Salerno handed Er Cervellone a pen and paper napkin, telling him to sign his name. This Er Cervellone did, and G.V. Salerno congratulated him for being "the first new comrade." The other patrons laughed, but G.V. Salerno folded the napkin into his shirt pocket and solemnly announced that, as the first recruit, Er Cervellone would also have the honour of buying him (G.V. Salerno) another Campari. This Er Cervellone did.

Paternoster

That somebody at the Viminale should have collected the imbecilic humourlessness of 'Paternoster' was astounding; even Josselin's hungriest informants wouldn't have approached him with such nonsense without a justified fear of getting cuffed around the ears. But Paternoster's tragic notion of information also jibed with the picture of Giorgio Salerno provided by his brother: a man whose beliefs had been reduced to the glib.

And beyond that?

I looked up from the dossier and made a perfect pinch of my cigarette butt through the window into the alley. Beyond that, of course, were all the empty apartments and condominiums the glib real estate broker Giorgio Salerno probably had at his disposal for concealing a body.

157

Codella didn't like the idea, but couldn't dismiss it out of hand, either. At least he entertained it enough to order a record of Giorgio's holdings in the city and then, after he had perused the short list of eight officially unoccupied apartments, to leave me in his office for a half-hour while he went down the hall to confer with his superiors. When he came back, he was wincing like a man who had been warned of professional torments if he was mistaken.

"No warrants yet."

"Why not?"

"Because we don't have enough justification for them is why not. Because we still don't know Mariani is even missing and because we don't like Frenchmen coming in here with their suspicions about our prominent citizens. But mostly because the people down the hall don't want them yet. There are other ways to test the waters."

"Plumbers?"

Codella flicked at the bottom of his beard. "Exterminators. We seem to have only their uniforms at the moment."

"Then it's done. We have him."

"Your confidence is staggering, Frenaud."

"It's the wedding. Can't you see that? That's what triggered everything. There's no way he wanted cousin Patti and all she represented coming over to ruin it."

He repressed a reply and reached over for his phone. But as he began issuing the orders that would put his exterminators into action, I realised I wanted one last favour from him. "Would it be a problem if we waited an hour or so? Maybe I can spend the time usefully with the brother."

"How? At best he's a *cafone* who doesn't know what's happened under his nose. But suppose he's been Salerno's willing accomplice in this little play of yours?"

"I think I can take care of myself with somebody who's what, almost old enough to be my grandfather? On the other hand, I can have a little chat with him, you can call me at his place to say your exterminators haven't found anything, and I can ride to the wedding with him."

Codella gave me one of his sad smiles. "You'd really hate getting that kind of call, wouldn't you?"

I was past caring at his digs at my personal involvement. What was important was that he gave me my hour. As I walked out of the Viminale and headed for the taxi rank across the street, I felt strangely civilian about everything. Mario Salerno was no longer my responsibility; it was that of the Italian police. I don't know why that suddenly felt as though it had been my goal all along, but it did.

Giorgio Salerno lived in a five-story high-rise in the middle of a somnolent street in the Monte Mario district. I only had to mention Salerno's name to get past the woman's voice on the lobby intercom. I assumed the voice was of Giorgio's wife, referred to in his dossier as Daria Something.

What had I expected in Giorgio Salerno? Rough edges, I suppose; not exactly a blue-collar labourer with a five o'clock shadow and meat hooks for hands, but at least someone whose white shirts were too wide at the collar and who was physical about showing prospective buyers his apartments, banging on pipes and kicking at woodwork to demonstrate their solidity. I was wrong, of course. The man standing in his doorway as I stepped out of the elevator might have been a university professor. Bright-eyed, stern-faced, he had an impeccably combed white mane. Instead of a white collar too wide around the neck, he wore a fashionable striped blue shirt and narrow burgundy tie; the tie was closed tightly by a gold collar pin. If appearances alone counted, Giorgio Salerno, not his brother, would have been the academician in the family.

"Can I help you?"

I was so taken aback I didn't see the years on the man until I was standing within range of a lemon-scented cologne. "I'm an acquaintance of Mario's," I said, taking in the soft throat skin and sloped shoulders. "I think we're going the same place at three o'clock."

It sounded atrocious even to me, but he smiled with curiosity and waved me into the apartment. "*Avanti, avanti!*"

I was ushered into a dining room consisting of a polished table and two ceiling-high sideboards bursting with silverware and elaborately flowered crockery. "Nothing's gone wrong?"

"No, no. Mario just thought since we were both going from the same neighbourhood and I don't have a car, we might go together."

He squinted in disbelief. "This was Mario's idea?"

Before I had to answer, Daria Salerno, a short, roly-poly woman in a housecoat but with her hair and makeup ready for a wedding, came out of a hall separating the dining room from the living room beyond it. "*Buon Giorno,*" she said, making it sound like a question.

"My wife Daria, Signor...?"

"Frenaud. Robert Frenaud."

Salerno had already decided something was wrong. "Signor Frenaud is a friend of Mario's. Mario suggested we go to the wedding together."

The woman's tentative smile evaporated; as she walked the length of the table to shake hands, she was hard pressed not to roll her eyes over to her husband. "Well, it would have been nice if Mario had told us something! But that's not his way, is it? How do you know Mario, Signor...?"

"Frenaud," I said, determined to tell the truth the rest of the way. "We met in an official capacity. I'm a policeman, in Rouen, in France. I ran into Mario last night and he invited me today."

Salerno had food for thought, she more reason for suspicion. "That sounds very mysterious."

"What's mysterious," he snapped, "is why you've been getting dressed for three hours and still aren't ready to go."

"And I suppose you're going in those pants?"

"That will take a second. *Per carita*, Daria!"

She thought about drawing me into another crack at his expense, then thought better of it. "There's coffee on the stove," she said, swinging her hips back into the hall. "Offer some to Signor Frenaud."

"*Ciao*, Daria!"

I felt ridiculous for being there. The idea that these elderly, bickering people were mixed up in the murder of Patricia Mariani was ludicrous beyond words. I hoped my father's spirit was hovering nearby to see the practical results of 'taking an extra minute'. "I'm sorry, Signor Salerno. There seems to be some kind of misunderstanding."

He pulled a chair out from the gleaming dining table. "Sit, sit."

"I think I should just…"

He waved his arm imperiously at the chair opposite the one he took. "Sit and tell me how I've disappointed you." His tone was a growl, but not a completely disapproving one. "It's written all over your face. Which means one of two things, Mario or some police dossier. Since you sound like you barely know my brother, I'd say your expectations came from one of those Viminale files that aren't supposed to exist. Don't be so surprised. I'm old, not senile. And I'm glad to meet you."

It seemed like tact to take the chair. "Glad?"

He began flexing his right arm. "Whatever you want from me, it was important enough to get you up here. It's been a long time since you people paid attention to me. The mental invalids who run this country must be getting very desperate."

"I assure you…" He looked offended, and I agreed with him. "All right. There's an inquiry that involves your brother. I thought you might be of some help."

"Something Mario did in France?"

"Here in Rome."

161

He turned his puzzlement back to his arm. "Always stiffens up around this time in the afternoon. Are you saying Mario's marrying a woman dangerous to the NATO alliance and all the capitalist democratic forces? More power to them. Whatever good it does these days."

"This has nothing to do with NATO," I said stupidly.

"Good. I don't count on too many things anymore, Frenaud, but I have to admit I've resigned myself to leaving this world in more or less the same condition I've lived in it."

His tartness made it easier. "Do you know Patricia Mariani?"

He glanced up speculatively, then instantly corrected himself and went back to his arm. "Of course I do. She's a cousin. Mario lived with her family in America. What about her?"

"She's disappeared."

"Yes?"

"Here in Italy."

"You're talking in riddles, Frenaud. Mariani is not to be found in Italy and the French police are looking for her? This European Community becomes stronger every day."

The plain white clock on the sideboard next to him said I had used up fifty of the minutes Codella had given me. "I was just hoping you might have seen her and had some idea where she was going."

In the light coming in from the windows at the far end of the living room he had the same liquid eyes as his brother only with more redness, more tiredness. "If she was in Rome, she'd be here to see Mario, not me. And I think you know that. I've met the woman exactly once, at least ten years ago when she came here with some *mascalzone,* who called himself a poet. She sat right there in that chair you're sitting in while her friend insisted on putting goggles on Daria, then turning on this little box that was supposed to make her see coloured waves and relax. Daria didn't relax for two weeks afterward! The two of them had one drink, then I threw them out. A cousin from America she kept calling herself. But she couldn't even say hello in Italian and expected us to speak in English. That was enough for me of my cousins from America."

"Your brother wasn't with her?"

"He was in America at the time. But what are you looking for? Why aren't you asking him these questions?"

"I don't think he'd answer them."

He let the words fall on the table, then, after a moment, leaned over with his right hand and wiped at a spot where they might have landed. "This is something serious?"

"I think so."

Something dropped on the floor in an inside room. "Something has happened to Mariani?"

"That's right."

"Nothing surprising about that. She looked like somebody heading for trouble." He hiccoughed a laugh. "Sat there that night telling me she was going to get rid of her poet with the goggles and wave box and marry Mario. Said it like her poet was in another room, not right next to her! At least that's what I think she was saying. Kept making all these hand gestures, like I was an Indian in one of those cowboy movies."

"Did you believe her?"

"Why not? Sounded like something stupid enough for Mario to do." He shook his head. "No, not even he would have been that stupid. I really thought she was a little mad. But I humoured her and her friend for a half-hour before I threw them out. When you sit at this table, Frenaud, you get to say just so many stupid things, then I throw you out."

"We think Mario knows something about Mariani's disappearance."

"So? Is it against the law to disappear? Disappear from whom? Is it against the law for other people to keep their secret?" I wanted a cigarette, but didn't dare move for one. "I was against Mario going to America. And I was happy when he called to say he was marrying Carla. She's on television all the time. Another one playing games with these charlatans filling their pockets running back and forth from the state network to private networks. And she's got a brother who goes around calling himself a 'new politician' because he doesn't know how to spell the word fascist. But I don't care about any of that. She has brains. She's a woman of quality."

"I know. I've met her."

He sat back so hard his chair creaked; his glibness had circled back into his own ears and he didn't like hearing it. "Between being against him going to America and being happy for his marriage... there should have been more for all the years in between, I suppose."

I was startled to see another five minutes gone on the clock. "You've reconciled your differences, then?"

"Reconciled?", he glared. "What's there to be reconciled about? He's always done *cazzi suoi*, and so have I. We're not combatants, Frenaud. Now, am I supposed to sit here all day until you tell me how Mario is connected to this famous disappearance?"

I had assumed he had understood. "We think she's dead."

"That's not what I asked."

The second part felt easier. "We think Mario killed her."

He flinched, but barely. "And you people who are doing all this grand thinking, why do you think he's done that?"

"Because she threatened him here. Because she represented something from over there he wanted to keep over there."

"So he just took some knife or gun...?"

"We don't have those details yet."

"But when you stepped off that elevator, you were expecting me to help fill them in for you, that it?"

I got to my feet, but his glare stayed with me. "I was wrong to impose, Signor. We have to be scrupulous, and sometimes that gets out of hand. In any case, it's now a matter for your own police. Excuse the intrusion."

He could only shake his head in disbelief. "Why don't you astonish me? Why do I just sit here and listen to you like you're saying the most natural things in the world?"

"Perhaps somewhere in the back of our minds we're all aware of what the people closest to us are capable of."

"*That*'s what you came here to blame me for?"

"No, no such thing…"

"Who are you, Frenchman? Who are you to walk in here with your shit cynicism and your 'we think this' and 'we think that?' What do 'we' know about me or my brother or anything else? You presumptuous bastard!"

I started for the door, cursing the moment in the hotel room that I had picked up the man's dossier and the evening my father had caught me tinkering with One-Two-Three. "As I say, it was a regretful mistake."

"Like hell it was. Your pound of flesh is what you came for. Or are you so far gone you really believe I go around abetting murder? You people never give up, do you? You hate life so much you can't even be satisfied to dance around on the rubble of the Great Soviet Peril. You're too busy crying over the loss of your alibi, afraid your frauds and squalors will become too visible." He thrust out his jaw mockingly. "Al-Qaeda, these Taliban lunatics in Afghanistan, maybe these genocide tribes in Africa, invest in them, Frenaud. Use them right and maybe they'll see you through all the way to your pension. Viva Iraq!"

The phone on the living room coffee table gave off a muffled buzz that was more piercing than a normal jangle. I told myself it was too soon for Codella. Salerno didn't seem to hear it at all; he sagged down in his chair, squinting at what might have been some new source of pain in his right forearm. "It must be nice knowing everything," he said. "I knew everything fifty, sixty years ago, too. Knew it all and then outsmarted myself. My mistake wasn't that I was wrong, Frenaud, it was that I was mainly interested in being right. If I had been Mario back then, I would have told me to go to hell, too."

For a moment, I thought the ringing had stopped of its own volition; but then I heard the wife's voice in a back room.

"He was my younger brother, Frenaud. He even admired me for a while. One day I caught him playing soldier in the piazza with the other kids. They were running in and out of the market stalls with chunks of wood for guns. Mario was playing *me*! The partisan hero, shooting down all the Nazis. He was never practical, you see. And I certainly wasn't. Only my mother was. She was practical enough for an army." He rubbed at his weak arm. "Not being practical, yes, in that we've been accomplices. In wanting to believe we could make ourselves and everybody else more convenient by reducing us and them to mental particles. But in the garbage you have in your head, whatever particles *you've* broken us down to, in that we've never seen eye to eye on anything."

High heels were coming down the hall. "But you're still not shocked by what I'm saying," I got in quickly.

His mockery came back. "Shocked? Do you know what I've been accused of over the years, Frenaud? What cretins like you have painted me as to justify their grovelling fears? So the latest one with a French accent walks into my apartment and says my brother has killed our cousin, and I'm supposed to accept that without question, like I'm hearing some sacred truth? You're very smug, Frenchman."

Daria Salerno stood in the hall between the dining room and living room. She wore a silk, grey dress and pearls. As she stared at her husband in consternation, she opened and closed her hand for some visible leverage in front of her chest. "It's for Signor Frenaud. A Signor Codella. You can take it over there. I left the extension off."

I had no choice but to move off my spot to the living room. "What is this about Mario?" she asked Salerno as I went by.

"Nothing."

"I heard you say…"

"You didn't hear anything. Are you ready yet?"

As I picked up the phone on the coffee table, my eyes fell on a wall cabinet that hadn't been visible from the dining room. The cabinet's four shelves were crammed with photographs. Even halfway across the room I recognized a six- or seven-year-old Mario Salerno standing at the elbow of Giorgio, then looking around twenty. Mario was frowning, either because the sun was in his eyes or because Giorgio's hand was too heavy on his shoulder.

"Via Palestrina 62. Come now."

The terseness of the order froze me. "You promised me time…"

"I'm giving you twenty minutes to get here," Codella said even more officiously. "There's a car waiting downstairs for you. I'd prefer you not be there when my men pick up the brother for questioning. This is going to be complicated enough, Robert. Please leave now and go downstairs to the car I've sent. When you get here, you'll have five minutes to make notes for your report to old Blanc. Then it's over. *A presto.*"

The click came before I could reassure him that Giorgio Salerno had been extraneous to whatever his exterminators had discovered. It would have been useless anyway; in Codella's place, I would have insisted on picking up the brother for questioning, too.

Back in the dining room, Daria Salerno was still standing next to Giorgio waiting for him to look up and fill her in on our conversation. He was waving her quiet with his bad arm.

167

Via Palestrina 62 was chaos. The street teemed with enough officers for a terrorist siege. And not a single one of them seemed concerned about the neighbourhood people who were milling around the building entrance. In the thirty seconds it took my driver to crawl the last few metres; I made out two people slipping inside to the lobby. No less appalling, I got all the way to the elevator before an officer intercepted me for credentials.

Upstairs, the thick rot wasn't just in the air, it was in the very floors, walls, and ceilings of the apartment. Somebody had had the idea of spraying the totally evacuated front rooms with a peppermint deodorant, and that had only made it worse: a layer of sweet chemicals atop a layer of putrefaction. As I made my way to the back of the apartment, a bespectacled officer watched me edgily for a reaction. I made a show of covering my mouth and nose with my handkerchief, and he smiled at me bleakly.

Unlike the front rooms, the bedroom was still furnished down to the carpet. Aerosol cans lined the bureau. There were so many of them and of so many scents, that it occurred to me they had been brought in not by Codella's people but by Salerno himself. Codella was standing next to the bed in conference with a forensics man. I felt better seeing their exaggerated casualness a couple of feet away from the bagged body on the bed: Even with cotton in their nostrils, they were working as hard as I was to disguise their disgust. Without breaking off his conversation, Codella nodded it was all right for me to take a closer look at the body.

Through the plastic Patricia Mariani seemed more preserved than decomposed. She had been a heavy woman, certainly heavier than I had imagined her from Salerno's writings and Jill Faber's stories. She wore a rose skirt and support hose of an identical colour. Why had she been wearing stockings in the middle of summer? Had Salerno put them on her out of some fetish after killing her? Or had she been so self-conscious about her thick legs she had tormented herself with heavy clothes even in the heat?

Her white blouse covered a broad back. There was a chain wedged into the mottled back fold of her neck. The hair was dirty blonde, cut short. There were no signs of blood or even of a struggle.

"Drugs."

The forensics man, a scarecrow with a pencil moustache, was addressing me across the bed, apparently at Codella's prompting. It took me a long moment to understand the hint of ironic satisfaction on Codella's face. But then I recalled his laments about Salerno's influential friends. "Obviously, we'll wait for the autopsy," he told me, taking over for the forensics man. "But we seem to have more than one possibility here."

I couldn't get the words out fast enough. I was almost unintelligible even to myself. "But he did it! You can't pretend...!"

As though on cue, the forensics man took a last look at the body and hurried from the room. Codella ambled over to the window and lit a cigarette. It dawned on me what the "five minutes" he had promised on the phone were to be spent on. "This isn't suicide, and you know it."

"No, Inspector Frenaud, I know nothing of the kind," he said, keeping his back to me. "Nor do you. That's why we'll do an autopsy and why we'll have both Salernos in for questioning. I've sent people for them already."

"But everything he's done over the last few weeks..."

"Everything he's done over the last few weeks can also be explained by a man beyond himself with grief and guilt. Oh, I accept all your premises about his interest in this dead painter and even his dark designs on these other people he's been tracking all over Europe. But that doesn't necessarily mean homicide." When he turned back, he gave off the same sharp impatience he had flashed in the restaurant. "Does it?"

"You mean it can't possibly be homicide because then you'd have to step on some of those toes you want to avoid. And I gather even his new wife is bringing more political connections to him."

He nodded, almost contentedly. I had used up the one sally he was going to permit me. "There's an empty vial of gluthemide in the bathroom," he said smoothly. "We have to assume its contents are now in the deceased's stomach. How the pills got there will be the next step. Rest assured, Frenaud, we will get to the truth of the matter and announce our findings. It goes without saying we are grateful to you for guiding us this far. I'll be putting that in writing to old Blanc."

I waited for more, but he kept his piercing stare until he had to worry about his cigarette ash. He looked around for some kind of ashtray, then had to settle for the windowsill. "It works both ways, you know," he said. "You should keep an open mind, too. A man convulsed by a woman he's apparently wanted to keep as far away, but also as close, as the memory of his first affair. She invades his fortress. Worse, she invades it to discover he's about to take a step he's never taken before, commitment to another woman. He wants to believe he's finally made a decision like a mature man. She will hear none of it. She has depended on him too long, as much as he's depended on her. When he shows he's really serious, she gets the pills and kills herself one lasting act of spite in obligating him to explain her demise to people like you and me. But he isn't ready to explain anything to anybody, even himself. Maybe he actually begins to think of himself as her murderer. Then begins the grand play around Europe, the play up here in the mind, Frenaud, to wipe out that damned spot. And you, especially you, reassure him by going after him. He has never been so *indebted* to anyone in his fractured life before. *Addio*, Inspector."

170

He strode out to the front rooms, leaving me to gaze blindly at Patricia Mariani. Who, I realized, had already ceased to exist before I had ever met Mario Salerno.

I never saw Salerno again and, after about a week, couldn't find anything more to read about him. The autopsy verdict was that Mariani had killed herself with an overdose of gluthemide. Codella's official conclusion was that Salerno had been so distraught at discovering her body in the apartment, he had secured for her from his brother, that he had suffered something called 'an incipient nervous collapse'. The phrase did not exist in any of the reference books in my office and I suspected it existed in Codella's office only in the dossiers stacked against his walls. The wedding to Carla Vianello was postponed indefinitely, meaning either until Salerno completed a recovery programme in a psychiatric clinic outside Siena, until Vianello got over her shock, or until her brother stopped fuming that a Salerno in the Vianello family wouldn't help his political ambitions. Codella, who had the courtesy to call me before the announcement of the suicide verdict, predicted the marriage would never take place. He made it sound like a dubious achievement of mine.

The actual interrogation of Salerno produced little that hadn't become obvious. Again, Codella made sure I received a transcription to minimise my suspicions about his handling of matters. They weren't especially minimised, though I was able to cross one final *t* with Salerno's explanation of why Mariani had flown to Milan rather than Rome from New York. According to page thirty-four of the transcript:

MS: She knew I was busy chairing a conference on displaced persons in Europe. I had made it clear to her

on the phone I was going to be caught up in that the first few days she wanted to come. Patti never liked taking a back seat to anything, so she decided to take the flight to Milan and work her way south, figuring I would be finished by the time she arrived in Rome. There was no talking her out of coming altogether.

But there had been none of the usual late evenings together when she had come, either.

MS: I asked Giorgio for the loan of an apartment that was away from the centre of the city and that had at least a bed in it. I asked him for favours so seldom he sent me the keys without a single question. When Patti phoned from the train station, she was annoyed I wasn't going to put her up. By the time the cab had taken her to Via Prenestina, she was in full diva rage. I met her there and told her all about Carla. She thought I was joking at first, then, when she realized I was serious, insisted on meeting Carla. I told her that wasn't going to happen. She could stay at the apartment for as long as she needed it, but I had no time for entertaining her. She started telling me about a musician or somebody who had taken her for money in New York, but I didn't want to hear it. It might have been true, it might have been she who had taken the money. I had heard so many stories like it before. I told her I wasn't interested. That's when she began to believe me.

There was another question not put directly to him, but that had teased me all the way home to Rouen: Why Carla Vianello? Why had he suddenly found in her the strength to break off with cousin Patti? What I had to take as an answer was something he said in another context:

MS: Do you know what loneliness is? It's about not knowing somebody who shares some of your assumptions. Not all of them, just some of them. Carla had stories I knew. I had stories she could even finish for me sometimes! How was that possible, I wondered. We had grown up as differently as any two people could, not to mention our age difference, but we had common stories. Witty stories, bizarre stories, sometimes just embarrassing stories. We had lived them completely independent of one another, but there it was anyway, that common ground. Without knowing it, both of us had been living beyond only ourselves, after all. We were unique precisely because we weren't!

I did all my paperwork for Blanc, and he seemed reasonably happy with the results. His major objection was that I had labelled the report SALERNO, MARIO. It came back to me with a red-penned correction of KELLER, GEORGE and the scribbled note: "As far as I am aware, the man who leaped from the window at the Flamant was named Keller, not Salerno. We should really try to remember the names of the victims we are investigating. It will make it infinitely easier for future researchers of our files. They will thank us for our scrupulousness, as I now thank you for yours."

Over my chagrin, Blanc's reprimand reminded me of the Keller sketch I had not sent to the U.S. Consulate. I found it in my middle drawer and took another look at it. The American painter was very literally a dead issue, the man would have never been mistaken for Degas, and the mailman in the sketch appeared eternally frozen in the midst of some gripe probably common to every mailman in the world. Whatever George Keller had seen in the man had been a uniqueness, impervious to his own mediocre abilities. Without the GK at the bottom of the paper, the study could have been done by me, Odile, or anybody else in Rouen.

I started to toss the drawing into my basket, then looked at the GK again. Degas or not, George Keller had still been George Keller, had known it was George Keller sketching the patrons at the café across the street from the Flamant, had known it was George Keller stepping out on the ledge of the hotel, had known it was George Keller plunging down into the courtyard. George Keller had killed himself in total awareness of his own identity. It hadn't been somebody else to do those things or bear the blame for his having done them. Dead *and* alive, George Keller had been a whole. For a chilling moment, that felt like an unfathomably more important feat than stopping Mario Salerno's marriage.

The night after Roger and Janine finished summer school, Rachel served her most elaborate dinner in months. The mushroom soup, roast lamb, glazed vegetables, and Provencal tarts were her way of saying some money was once again available for spending in ways *she* wanted. Jens Madsen's visit helped her say it.

Madsen had been in Paris more than a week researching his pet project on so-called sociopath s. I suppose I shouldn't have been surprised when he called to say that he had secured official time to ferret through the Sorbonne and other dusty Parisian libraries or that the Danish Foreign Ministry was on the verge of underwriting his musings with some funds; after all, we had met originally because of another flimsy academic exercise. What did put me off was that he had waited until the day he was scheduled to return home to declare his presence in France. I thought I might have expected a little more notice from him, if not an invitation for me and Rachel to join him in Paris for a day or so.

In any case, he did find some hours for Rouen and, as soon as I got over my peevishness at his failure to call earlier, I was happy for his visit. Rachel, too. Unlike some of our other dinner guests, Jens was never one to compliment the cook and then ignore her for all but the most generic conversation. On the contrary, his tales of Scandinavian mayhem, opinions of new films and old politics, often seemed more directed at Rachel than at me, and he courted her reactions assiduously. "He thinks I'm more of a real person than you are," she had said blithely one night in Jens's guest room in Virum. "How can he possibly trust the thinking of another policeman? He already has those opinions." As miffed as I had been at that sally, I had come to realise (and was hoping again as Rachel brought out the dessert) that some of our most passionate nights had followed an evening with our Danish friend. The more genteel he was, the more both of us needed to reclaim something more urgent in ourselves, to confirm we would never grow too philosophical or meditative about one another.

For his part, Jens wore his archive digging on his face. I had never seen him so ashen, and told him so. "Not just the research," he agreed readily.

"Denise Rosen has been making you wish you could have your middle-aged crisis back?"

He laughed without enthusiasm, even before Rachel's more evident interest in his answer. "Yes, we see each other, but I'm fast losing ground to *Fear and Trembling*. But there's been all that business around the airport too. I think that's why they gave me this week off. I wrote so many reports contradicting one another I *had* to be right at some point."

"You can make the case against these Swedes and Norwegians?"

He nodded. "A reprieve for everyone."

"Then why don't you sound reprieved?" Rachel asked.

He lit his pipe behind a nod. "All that venom in the newspapers and television, the uneasiness in the streets, mobilising the armed forces, maybe I would have liked seeing all that poison channelled into something we could have drawn a lesson from. But no. In the end we're able to blow it across the borders of our neighbours. Where it now remains as a pollution the next wind will blow back over us. I'm afraid that just isn't neat enough for this grey mind."

I couldn't help thinking of Codella. "Take solace your courts won't call those people killed in the bank suicides."

Jens glanced at Rachel above his lighter, then capped it loudly. As if by prearranged signal, Rachel stood up with the announcement that she needed to check something with Roger. I remembered her whispering with Madsen in the living room while I had been getting ice in the kitchen.

"Ever consider the possibility Mariani *did* kill herself?" he asked as soon as Rachel had left.

"You've been talking to Madame Frenaud."

"She says this thing is still gnawing at you."

"Of course it is," I said angrily. "She didn't have to make a secret of it. I don't need a shoulder to cry on, Jens. I need somebody in authority in Rome to admit two and two make four."

"*You* need, Robert?"

"A manner of speech. Don't go professional on me."

"Some would say you're the one who should go more professional."

I had no answer to that. He was right, as Blanc, Rachel, Josselin, and who knew how many others had been right. I finished my coffee.

"Of course it can be frustrating," he said finally. "I confess that after putting together everything you told me and then making some inquiries of my own... Well, what did you expect I would do, Robert? You got me so far out into the water I could hardly pretend not to be wet. And I have to say everything I learned was more or less what you said."

"More or less?"

"The facts were exactly as you said. And like you always told me you did, I followed those facts back..."

"And?"

He shrugged. "And came up with possibilities. Of course if I'd made the mistake you've always liked to warn me about, letting myself be led by some preconceived notion..."

"Sometimes your condescension isn't appealing, Jens."

"And sometimes it's warranted," he said curtly.

We were as close as we had ever been to a serious argument. For that alone I despised Mario Salerno: He and his American drugheads simply weren't worth it.

"More coffee," I decided. He nodded promptly. "Well, maybe you'll end up getting more out of this than anyone. At least Salerno should give you a chapter or two on your sociopathic personalities."

"Salerno? Hardly."

"Why not?"

He pulled his refilled cup into him. "Because he isn't one, not in the least. Oh, I admit I thought so for a while. What I bored you with on our drive out to the airport. But if anything, Mario Salerno sounds like the opposite, somebody who has made a very tortured job of trying to preserve history. Wherever he lashed out in the name of vindication, here or over there, he found a very identifiable piece of himself. Artificial maybe, but identifiable."

Rachel was going at it with Roger. All I could hear clearly through a couple of doors was the word *clothes*. Could that have been why he had called me at the office that day?

"For a true sociopathic type, Robert," Madsen said, amused, "I think I'd be much more interested in you."

I laughed, telling myself it was what he expected of me. My cigarette smoke smelled harsh and thin compared to the layered sweetness coming from his pipe.